"Her Chr

The Ging

By Laura Ann

HER CHRISTMAS BAKER

First edition. November 30, 2020.

Written by Laura Ann.

DEDICATION

To my child who lives for telling jokes.
Your humor is an essential part of life.
Never stop laughing.

ACKNOWLEDGEMENTS

No author works alone. Thank you, Brenda.
You make it Christmas every time
I get a new cover. And thank you to my Beta Team.
Truly, your help with my stories is immeasurable.

PROLOGUE

The tinkle of the small bell on the top of the door was a cheery sound against the cold winter day, and Emory couldn't help but smile. She stepped inside the small space and shivered at the change in temperature. Along with the warmth, smells permeated the intimate space and gave an immediate feeling of home.

"Welcome to The Boardwalk Bakery." A friendly voice came from the front. "How can I help you today?"

Emory shook herself from her wandering thoughts and walked away from the door. She smiled at the young clerk. "Just thought I'd grab something sweet while I did a little work."

"You're in the right place," the clerk said with a smile. "I'm Jennifer and I can personally vouch that everything in the display case is delicious."

Emory's smile grew. "I have your word, huh? That's about as good as it comes."

The teenage girl laughed. "Maybe I should just admit that I've eaten everything here and can't seem to stop."

"That's a recommendation I can get behind," Emory agreed. She looked down at the beautiful display case and felt a ping of jealousy. *Someday,* she assured herself. *Someday I'll have my own bakery, and I won't have to deal with egotistical head chefs, and no one else will take credit for my creations.* "These look delicious," she said to the clerk.

"Thank you," a deep, slightly accented voice said from behind her.

Emory jerked upright and spun on her heel.

"Oh, hey, Mr. Harrison," Jennifer chirped. "I thought you'd gone home for the day."

Emory couldn't seem to make her mouth work. The cold outside was completely forgotten as she stared at the tall, dark and handsome stranger in front of her. His hair was just long enough to sweep across his eyes, which were nearly the color of stainless steel. He was lean, but strong, if the fit of his long T-shirt was anything to go by. But what caught Emory's attention the most was the apron tied around his waist and covered with what appeared to be frosting and cinnamon.

"I just went next door for a moment," the man said to Jennifer, though his eyes stayed on Emory. He nodded toward the case. "Pick what you like. It's on the house."

The richness of his voice was as silky as a good pot de créme, and filled her with warmth before his words penetrated the fog of attraction she was experiencing.

"Uhh..."

A slow smile crept across his well-formed lips. "Where are my manners?" he murmured, then stepped forward with his hand out. "I'm Antony Harrison."

Emory shook her head, feeling a spurt of anger at her reaction to this man. She didn't have time to be ogling anyone, no matter how good-looking they were. She had come to Seagull Cove to help in her grandmother's kitchen and to win the gingerbread competition. When Grandma had fallen a few months ago, the inn had been closed and the workers let go. But now, they were opening just in time for Christmas, and Emory, plus two of her cousins, were there to help out until after the holidays.

Emory had been hoping this was going to be her chance to shine for a moment before going back to Seattle and slowly dying in the dregs of hotel restaurant work. "Emory Mason," she said, shaking his hand firmly.

"Oooh, you're one of the granddaughters," Jennifer drawled from behind her.

Emory turned, her eyebrows up. "Uh, yeah. How did you know that?"

Jennifer shrugged and tucked a piece of blonde hair behind her ear. "Everyone's been talking about you, and it's not like Claire has been quiet." Jennifer giggled. "I think the whole town knows you three are coming."

"The question is," Antony said, drawing Emory's attention again, "which one are you?" He put a hand on his chin. "The teacher, the reporter, or the baker?" His eyes went from Emory's head, down to her toes and back.

She had to lock her knees, the heat in the already warm bakery shooting up a notch. "Which do you think I am?" she asked with a tilt of her chin.

That slow grin came back, doing delicious things to her belly. "With that little bit of bite, I would normally say you were the reporter."

"I hear a 'but' in there," Emory said with forced politeness.

"But...I also saw the way you were looking at my display." He smirked. "One baker should always be able to recognize another."

Emory stood tall, her chin still in the air. "Surely a taste test is the best way to get to know another baker, don't you think?"

His eyes sparkled at the challenge. "I agree." He leaned forward a little, as if the conversation were just between the two of them. "In that case, why don't you let me choose something for you?"

Emory's competitive side jumped to attention and joined with the indignation that was already simmering at her unwanted attraction. "Go ahead. It'll be interesting to see what you think is worth my time."

Antony chuckled low and tilted his head in acknowledgement.

Jennifer whistled low under her breath. "It's getting hot in here," she muttered.

Emory stepped back, breaking the tension between her and Antony. "Actually, maybe I better be heading out. I have a lot of work to do today." Jennifer's remark had made Emory realize she was pushing things a little too far, especially with a stranger. She cleared her throat and began to back toward the door. "I'll have to try your treats another time."

"Hold on," Antony said, his tone commanding enough to stop her in her tracks. He walked around the counter and grabbed a small box, then filled it with pastries before walking it back to Emory. "You can try these when you have a break." He grinned. "And believe me, you'll want to try them."

Emory pinched her lips together. *Good-looking or not, I am so sick of egos.* "I'll pass, thanks."

Antony shook his head and continued to hold out the box. "I'm offering you a chance to test out your competition."

Emory frowned. "Why would you be my competition?"

His eyebrow rose. "Your grandmother said you plan to put in an entry to the gingerbread village."

Understanding hit. "You're entering as well."

He nodded. "Absolutely." He winked. "And I intend to win."

She snatched the box. "Thanks for the warning," she snapped, then held her head high as she went to the door. "But I'll warn you in return...my grandmother has been the reigning champion for ten years. I don't plan to let her reputation die."

Antony stood, watching her go with a confident smile and his hands in his pockets. "Let the games begin."

Pretending the picture he made wasn't the least bit enticing to her, Emory sniffed and stormed out the door. She almost threw the beautiful blue box in the trash on her way to her car, but caught herself at the last minute. *He's right,* she grudgingly admitted. *Tasting his food will let me know what I'm up against.*

As if the pressure she felt to win the competition wasn't already heavy enough, now she had a jerky baker to contend with. "A hot jerky baker," she grumbled to herself, then shook her head. "Who cares what he looks like, or even if he's single. He's my competitor and that's all there is to it."

ANTONY WATCHED THE stunning woman leave his shop in a huff, and he couldn't help but laugh a little. Seeing the sparks in her eyes as he teased her was the best way to start his day. He turned when he heard a loud huff, to see Jennifer with her hands on her hips.

"You're ridiculous, you know that?" she asked.

Antony nodded, still smiling wide. "Probably, but that was more fun than I've had in a long time."

Jennifer threw up her hands. "Why do guys think irritating a girl is funny? It only makes us angry."

"Ah...but anger can turn to something else when cultivated right," he said, pointing a finger at his employee.

Jennifer snorted. "Yeah, it's called hate."

"The line between hate and love is thin, little Jennifer."

She rolled her eyes in true teenage fashion. "Asking her out would have served much better, Mr. Harrison. And she wouldn't have stormed out of here as if she couldn't wait to get away from you. You just made yourself the enemy."

"No...I made myself front and center in her mind." He chortled and rubbed his hands together. "She'll be thinking about me all day."

"How to take your head off, maybe," Jennifer drawled, grabbing a rag and cleaning the already immaculate counter.

He laughed again. "Possibly. But I'm still front and center. Next time we meet, I'll push a little more."

"Next time you meet, she might refuse to speak to you."

Antony tsked his tongue and shook his head, heading toward the kitchen in the back of the building. "Oh ye of little faith. Trust me on this. I've been around the block a few times." He smiled when she grumbled again.

"That's what I'm afraid of," Jen muttered.

Antony ignored her last quip and went back to his sanctuary. Jennifer had been a major find in this small town he had made home. Or was trying to make home.

She was a homeschooled senior in high school, and was able to work all sorts of hours around her flexible schooling. She was friendly, a good worker, and had become like a little sister to him since hiring her six months earlier.

And the best part was she had welcomed him to Seagull Cove with no qualms about him being an outsider. While the tourists had no problem buying the goods from his shelves, the locals were another story. Antony had picked this town because his family had vacationed here when he was a child and he'd fallen in love with the misty mornings and cool, salty breezes. But small towns had history, and he wasn't a part of it.

The upcoming gingerbread competition, the very one that Claire Simmons' granddaughter was running in, was his chance to break into the inner circle of the cove. If he won, they'd have to pay attention to him, and maybe it would even open some doors for him to expand his small business.

The boardwalk had a candy shop, but there had been no bakery, making it perfect for Antony to come in and start one from the ground up. However, a business couldn't run on only six months of income, and the tourists visited far less in the winter than they did the summer.

Antony sighed and looked down at his flour-covered counter. He was good at what he did. Really good. But no one would ever know if they didn't give him a chance.

Reaching below the counter, he pulled up his sketch for his gingerbread house. It was going to be one of his best creations to date. He loved sculpting even more than he loved baking, and having the ability to combine the two was a bonus.

Pulling a pencil from his pocket, he went to work, perfecting the design. Or...at least he tried to. His mind was filled with a dark-haired, blue-eyed woman who was probably cursing him to high heaven right now.

Her thin build and medium height was just right for his six-foot frame, and the fire in her was more than attractive...it was completely enticing. Building his business had put Antony out of the dating scene for a while, and Claire's granddaughter seemed like the perfect place to step back in.

If she'll even speak to you after the way you egged her on, he thought. A grin crossed his face. "Well, I guess I'll just have to find a way to make her speak to me. It shouldn't be that hard."

CHAPTER 1

Emory sighed as she looked at the drawing in front of her. Her sketchings for her gingerbread house were beautiful, but she wanted something...more. Something spectacular. Something that would prove to her grandmother and the rest of Seagull Cove that her years of culinary school were worth every penny.

"Something that will be all mine," she muttered as she erased and began sketching again. She'd been at it for days, practically since she'd arrived in The Cliffside Bed and Breakfast, also known to the locals as The Gingerbread Inn.

Gingerbread Inn had been holding a gingerbread village competition for years and it had become a big draw for winter tourism, which was often scarce on the Oregon coastline that they resided on.

When Grandma Claire had refused to listen to reason about re-opening, Emory and two of her cousins, all of whom were in-between jobs at the moment, had come running to help. Hope, who was looking for a full-time position as a teacher, was playing the job of housekeeper. Isabella, or Bella, an independent journalist, was running the front desk and Emory, who had taken a sabbatical from her job in a hotel restaurant, was running the kitchen, along with the competition.

Her grandmother's beautiful works of art had won the grand prize for the last ten years in a row and Emory was determined not to let her down. Emory frowned for a moment as she thought about her competition. The far-too-handsome-for-his-own-good Antony Harrison. She snorted. "There's also Mrs. Pearson," she reminded herself.

The older woman had been gunning after Grandma Claire's title for years, and always seemed to come in second best. Last year, Mrs. Pearson had been gone during the holidays, but she was back now and more eager than ever to dethrone Claire Simmons.

The doorbell of the mansion rang and Emory ignored it, knowing Bella would handle it, but when a deep voice filtered into the kitchen area, Emory froze. She'd heard those dulcet tones, before and listening to them now reminded her that she wouldn't mind hearing them again.

Emory shook her head with a scowl. "Knock it off," she scolded. "He's competition, not dating material."

"Emory? Will you come out here, please?" Bella called.

"Crud," Emory whispered. Glancing in the microwave for a second, she tucked a stray hair behind her ear, wiped at her face with a towel, and straightened her shoulders. "It's probably not even him," she told herself. "I mean, he lives in town. Why would he be at the inn?"

"Well, well, well..."

Emory closed her eyes. *Crud, crud, crud.* When she opened them, Antony Harrison was smiling at her with a mischievous light in his eyes.

"We meet again, Miss Baker."

Bella's eyebrows were high, and her mouth formed an 'O', before she began to smile.

Great. Now Bella's got ideas in her head.

"Hello, Mr. Harrison," Emory said primly, folding her hands in front of her apron. "What brings you here?"

Antony looked amused at her formal words, but stepped aside to show a lovely middle-aged woman. "My mother is here for a few weeks to visit. I'm afraid I live above the bakery in a tiny apartment that cannot hold us both comfortably." His eyes went to Bella, then back to Emory. "She has a reservation."

"I thought you should meet the guests as they came in," Bella said sweetly.

Emory held back a glare. *I'll be asking you about that later,* she promised.

Bella's response was to bat her eyelashes. "The Harrisons would like a tour of the mansion. Do you think you could help them with that?"

Emory balked and stared wide-eyed at her cousin. "I'm working. Can't you do it?"

Bella shook her head. "I can't leave the desk. We've got a couple more people coming to check in sometime today."

"What about Hope?"

Bella shrugged. "I'm not sure where she is."

Mrs. Harrison sniffed. "It would appear you have a staff issue."

Great. She's even more snooty than her son.

"I'm sure they'll take care of us, Mother." His gray eyes bore into Emory's. "I've heard wonderful things about this inn." The edge of his mouth curled up. "And the women working here."

Emory clenched her teeth. *Manipulative jerk. He wants a tour? Fine. I'll give them a tour.* She pasted a fake smile on her face. "I'm sure I can step away from the kitchen for a few minutes." Waving her hand toward the grand ballroom, which was now a large sitting room, she bid them forward. "If you'll head this way, we'll start in the main room."

Antony's lips twitched as if he were holding back a smile, but he put his hand on his mother's lower back and led her where Emory directed.

"The house is over a hundred years old," Emory began, knowing the tour speech by heart. She'd heard it more times than she cared to as a child and teen. "If you'll notice the extra large mantel. It's original to the house, built from driftwood found on the beach, just a mile down the road."

For the next thirty minutes, Emory played the polite hostess, showing them every inch of the large mansion...almost.

"Antony, I am tired," Mrs. Harrison stated. "Take me to my room."

"Of course, Mother," he said kindly. Antony looked to Emory. "Thank you for the tour. It was very interesting."

Not for the first time, Emory wondered about his accent. His mother's was more pronounced and sounded Italian to Emory. But

Antony's was less audible and only seemed to show up on certain words. Rather than asking the question, however, Emory found relief in the fact that she was done being hostess.

"You're welcome. If you'll go through that door, you'll find the front desk and Bella will make sure you're settled." Spinning on her heel, Emory returned to her safe haven as quickly as she could without looking like she was running from anything or anyone.

Once in the kitchen, she blew out a long breath and shook out her arms and legs. Adrenaline was pumping through her system, though she wasn't sure why. It seemed as if all it took was to be in Antony's presence for her ridiculous hormones to go crazy.

That silky voice and handsome face were enough to make any woman swoon. Emory took a deep breath. "But I'm not just another woman," she reminded herself. "And I'm not here to meet a man. In fact, in this case. I'm here to beat him. I'm here to prove myself and show that I'm capable and worthy." She straightened her shoulders. "I'm Emory Mason. And I'm here to win."

ANTONY GOT HIS MOTHER settled in her room, then bounded back down the stairs. Now that he knew where Emory was, he wasn't quite ready to leave without speaking to her by himself. He'd been thinking about her often since her foray into his store. Her snapping blue eyes had never left his head or his daydreams.

Reaching the front desk, he leaned against the counter. "Hello, Bella."

Bella grinned and rested her chin on her hands. "Hello, Antony."

"I have a question for you."

"And I have one for you."

He raised his eyebrows. "Then I'll be the gentleman and let you go first."

Bella's grin widened. "How did you meet Emory? And what did you do to her?"

Antony chuckled and rubbed his jaw. "That's two questions."

She straightened and waved a hand in the air. "Tomato, tomahto." Bella folded her arms over her chest. "If you want my cooperation to find my reclusive cousin, then I'd suggest answering them."

Shock hit Antony, before he broke out in laughter. "You drive a hard bargain."

Bella shrugged. "I know how to get what I want."

He nodded. "Okay. But if you get two questions, then so do I."

"Fair enough."

"All right, I met Emory a couple of days ago when she stopped in my bakery for a bite to eat."

"Ahh...that explains a lot," Bella mused.

Antony shrugged. "She might not have enjoyed the fact that I said I was going to enter the gingerbread competition...and win."

Bella snorted her laughter. "Oh yeah...that would get her goat, for sure."

"Now." Antony smiled. "My turn."

Bella held up one finger. "No, she's not taken. In fact, she's been single for far too long."

"How—?"

"And two, she's in the kitchen." Bella winked. "And I'm guessing she didn't show you that on the tour."

Antony slowly shook his head, then slowly clapped his hands. "That was impressive."

Bella shined her nails on her shirt. "Journalist. We notice things."

"And you're obviously very good at it."

"I try."

"You succeed." Antony looked past her, trying to figure out where the kitchen might be.

"Through the great hall. Take the door in the far left corner."

"One day I'll have you do a psychic reading for me," he teased, heading in the direction she gave.

"You can't afford me," Bella retorted, her eyes on the binder in front of her.

Antony chuckled, but decided it was best to keep moving. Walking across the large ballroom, he spotted the door she had been referring to. As he got closer, he could hear the sweet sounds of pots and pans being used as well as the delicious smell of baking bread. Putting his hand on the door, he paused to take a fortifying breath.

He might have been out of the game for awhile, but right here, right now, he had every intention of getting back in.

He pushed open the door and bit his lip when he spotted Emory on her hands and knees, digging into the back of a lower cabinet. She was grumbling to herself and her frustration was evident.

"Where the heck is it?"

"Can I help?" Antony ventured, making his presence known.

Emory squeaked and jumped backward, landing hard on her seat.

He winced when the cabinet door slammed into the wall at her quick movements and her tailbone thudded against the hardwood floor.

"I should have known," she grumbled, shaking her head. "Why is it you seem to be at the root of all my problems?"

Antony put on his best smile. "I don't know what you're talking about."

Emory rolled her eyes and slumped a little before trying to stand up.

"Here. Let me." Antony rushed over and put out his hands, waiting patiently while she hesitated before taking his assistance.

"I suppose if you're going to give me a heart attack at such a young age, you should be around to take me to the hospital."

He chuckled, helping her rise to her feet. "I'm less worried about the heart attack and more worried about bruising." He grinned sheepishly when she rubbed her lower back and tailbone. "You all right?"

"Dandy," she snapped. Stretching her back a little, Emory turned her back on him and headed toward the oven, her movements stiff and awkward.

"I really am sorry," he said. "I wasn't trying to startle you. I just wanted to talk."

"Talk?" Emory spun and stared at him with her brow furrowed. "About what?"

Antony folded his arms and spread his stance to be more comfortable. "You."

Her anger disappeared, replaced by shock. "Why in the world do you want to talk about me?"

He shrugged and walked a little closer, resting his hip against the counter. "I thought it might be nice to get to know each other...baker to baker."

She stared a moment longer before snorting and shaking her head. "If this is your plan to distract me into losing the competition, it won't work." Emory tapped her temple. "I'm one of those super-focused people."

He grinned. "Good to know. What else can you tell me about you?"

Emory snapped her mouth shut. "Nope. Nope. Nope. This isn't happening." She turned and grabbed a pair of hot pads, opening the oven.

The smell of bread grew stronger and Antony's mouth watered as he watched her bring several loaves out onto the counter top. *She's good. That'll only make this all the sweeter.* "Where did you go to school?"

"Nope."

Antony's lips twitched. "How long are you here?"

"Nope."

"How many siblings do you have?"

"Nope."

"What's your favorite color?"

"Nope."

Antony couldn't help but smile widely. He liked her. A lot. He had always been a competitor, and finding an attractive woman who was also a challenge? Life couldn't get any better at the moment. *Other than winning that gingerbread competition.* "Your favorite dessert?"

"Not happening."

"Are you single?"

She paused at that one and glanced over her shoulder, staring intently, but not speaking.

Knowing he had pushed his luck enough, and wanting to leave her with something to think about, he winked. "Good to know." Ignoring her sputtering, Antony strutted out of the kitchen and back to the foyer. "Thanks, Bella!" he called out as he opened the door to leave.

"Anytime!" she called back with a laugh. "It's been a pleasure...I think."

Antony couldn't help but continue smiling and chuckling as he got in his car to go home. Life had just gotten very interesting and exciting and he was looking forward to more.

CHAPTER 2

"Where is it?" Emory growled, searching once again in the pantry. She tore through the shelves systematically, going through the entire place from top to bottom, but the nougat was nowhere to be found.

Pushing her hands through her hair, she let out a small shriek of frustration. "It can't be gone! I know I brought it with me."

The doorbell rang in the distance, but Emory ignored it. She'd been searching for two days straight and was starting to become frantic. The nougat she had saved up for, and kept specifically for the festival at Gingerbread Inn, was gone.

"Where could it be?" she whispered thickly, her throat closing with tears. "I know I brought it."

A deep voice filtered into the kitchen from the foyer and a fire lit under Emory. "Him," she said through clenched teeth. The man who had become the bane of her existence was here, and wasn't it convenient that her specialty treat from France was missing? And just after he checked his mother into the bed and breakfast two days ago.

Anger and suspicion began to boil inside her until she could no longer sit still. Jumping to her feet, she practically ran to the front entryway. "YOU!" she shouted, pointing a finger in his direction. "Where is it?"

Antony gave her a curious look. "What exactly are you looking for, Emory?" he asked smoothly, but there was a wariness to his tone.

"The candies I brought with me," Emory said through clenched teeth. Tears were beginning to sting her eyes, but she refused to let them fall. "The specialty ones I ordered from France." She stepped even closer to Antony, ignoring the little zing she got every time they were in close proximity. "They're missing."

Antony frowned, appearing truly concerned. "Did you leave them somewhere?"

"Absolutely not!" Emory defended. "I specifically remember bringing them with me."

"And you think my son would have what?" Mrs. Harrison interrupted. Emory had been so set on Antony, she hadn't realized the woman was in the room. "Stolen them?" Mrs. Harrison threw up her hands. "What kind of place is this?" she asked. "We come as guests and are accused of being thieves!"

Emory shook her head hard, refusing to back down. "I'm not accusing you of anything, Mrs. Harrison. Only your son." She turned back to him. "Only another baker would have known how expensive and special that nougat was. It can only be purchased in France, specifically around Christmas."

Antony's eyes were wide. "You have Nougat of Montelimar here? How the heck did you get it?"

"That doesn't matter," Emory said. She wasn't about to give away her source. "Give it back."

Antony put his hands up, acting innocent. "I had nothing to do with it disappearing," he said. "But I'd be happy to help you find it."

"I'm sure you would," Emory snapped.

"Okay..." Hope said, stepping in-between Emory and Antony. Emory blinked. She hadn't even known Hope was there. "I think maybe we all just need to calm down."

"I am perfectly calm," Antony said with a smirk. "I believe it is your cousin that has gotten her apron in a twist."

Emory growled softly. His nonchalant attitude was only blowing oxygen on the already raging flames inside of her.

"I'm serious, Em. You need to take a step back and calm down," Hope pressed.

Emory pinched her lips together and obeyed Hope's orders. She knew her cousin was right, but how could Antony stand there, acting like nothing mattered? How could he deny he was the most logical choice for being the thief?

"I don't think we need to stand around and listen to this." Mrs. Harrison sniffed. "This...woman...obviously has issues. We should just—"

"Not so fast, Mother," Antony inserted. "I want to hear what Emory has to say." He folded his arms and gave her a penetrating look. "After all, she's convinced I'm the cause of her distress, and I, for one, would like to know why."

Emory took a deep breath, trying desperately to keep a hold of her emotions, but she was losing the battle. She was already nearly crumbling under the weight of carrying on Grandma's legacy, and now this delicious man was messing her life up, and everything was falling apart like last year's Christmas cookie. "I brought some candies and desserts with me for the Christmas party and gingerbread competition. They were expensive, specialty treats, and now one of the best ones is missing." She turned to Hope mid-explanation. "Most people would never know how hard it is to get that nougat. Only another baker," she shot a glare at Antony, "would understand its importance and how difficult it is to get. Not to mention he's looking to win this year in order to push his business."

"So you think Antony what? Came in in the middle of the night and stole it?" Hope asked. "Emory, that's a pretty bold accusation."

"Hear, hear," Antony echoed. "First of all, there is no honor in winning by sabotaging someone else." He raised an eyebrow at Emory. "Secondly, why would I bother to sneak in in the middle of the night?" he asked cooly, stepping closer to Emory. "When I know that you would let me in at anytime, hm?"

"You arrogant—"

"What exactly is going on here?"

The entire group spun to see Bella with her hands on her hips and her foot tapping.

"There's a story here. I can smell it and somebody better tell it to me."

Hope pinched the bridge of her nose. "Not now, Bella."

"Yes, now." Bella marched up to the group. "With as loud as you all are, we're going to start getting complaints at the front desk, and I'm going to have to deal with it. Count this as me being preemptive."

"Emory's foreign candy is missing and she's accusing Antony," Enoch, the inn's handyman, said with a sigh. He shrugged when Hope looked at him incredulously. "What? Did you really think you would keep it from her? She's got a nose like a bloodhound."

Bella preened under the words. "Why, thank you."

Hope shook her head and turned back to Emory. "Em, unless you have some proof that Antony did something, then we need to back down. Do you have any proof?"

Emory deflated, knowing she was losing her ground. "No," she said flatly. "But I'm meticulous in how I organize my things. None of my stuff ever goes missing." She stared hard at Hope. "Ever. The nougat is gone. Which means someone took it."

"Okay." Hope nodded her head. "Why don't you, me, and Bella search for it just to see if somehow someone misplaced it. If that doesn't work, we'll focus on what to do next."

"Fine," Emory snapped, her eyes darting to Antony and back to Hope. "But no one else is allowed in my kitchen except you two."

"ABOUT TIME YOU SAW sense," Mrs. Harrison said. She walked to the front door. "Antony, we're late. We need to leave."

Antony reached for the door handle, then paused. Emory was really upset and he couldn't blame her. If something of his had gone missing, he'd have turned the world over for it. "You will let me know when you find it?" he asked.

"Why do you care?" she asked sullenly.

"Because believe it or not, I'm not the bad guy," Antony said, turning his body to face her fully. He wanted her to know he was serious. He'd hoped that after their last encounter, she was softening toward him a little, but obviously that wasn't the case. It seriously made him reconsider whether or not he wanted to get to know her. She was beautiful, yes, and an excellent baker, but nothing about this confrontation was giving him warm feelings. A challenge was only enticing when there was a good reward at the end, and Emory's anger wasn't what he had in mind.

Their eyes met and the air instantly heated up around them. Those light blue orbs seemed to draw him in against his will, and he knew he couldn't be done with her just yet. Inside that intensity was a woman needing to be seen. *Just imagine how someone with her amount of fire would give a man something to fight for.*

So instead of giving up, he decided to do what he did best. Pulling out his best 'Confident Italian Lover' persona that his Italian uncles had carefully taught him, Antony gave her a cocky smirk. "We both know you're attracted to me. Who can be a bad guy with this kind of hair?" He pushed a hand through his dark locks, seeming to enjoy the reaction he was getting from the other baker.

"Antony," his mother said with a tsk of her tongue while Emory gasped in outrage. He heard Hope groan, but Bella laughed out loud. "You must stop this now." His mother pulled open the door and grabbed his arm. "Enough of this tomfoolery. We go."

Antony let his mother drag him outside, still chuckling as he went. As far as shock value went, he'd hit the nail on the head. The problem was, that nail might have been in his coffin. His little stunt wasn't going to help his cause in exploring the chemistry between him and Emory.

He led his mother to his car and got her settled before hopping into the driver's seat.

"You like her," his mother stated baldly as they pulled onto the road.

Antony glanced at her before going back to the road. "I don't know yet."

His mother was quiet for a while before speaking again. "She...has spirit."

Antony grinned. His mother could be a difficult woman, but in the end...he knew she loved him. "She does," He nodded slowly. "It kind of reminds me of another woman I know."

She gave him a dry look.

Antony chuckled.

"So what are you going to do about her?"

Antony sighed. "I don't know. I find her attractive and I'm pretty sure she feels the same."

His mother snorted, as femininely as possible, of course.

"I also enjoy the fact that she and I have similar interests and that she's strong-willed."

"But..."

"But she seems to have decided she'd rather be a fighter than a lover." Antony rested his elbow on the window and leaned his head into his hand. "I'd love to keep pushing, but I'm not sure she'll let me."

The car was quiet for several minutes as he pulled into the parking lot of the restaurant he was treating his mother to for lunch. They went inside and were seated before she offered her advice.

"While I do not appreciate that she accused you of thievery," she pinned her son with a stare, "if you wish to get to know her, then you will have to do so in a way that leaves her no choice but to reciprocate."

"And how do you suggest I do that?" Antony asked, leaning back in his seat and folding his arms over his chest.

Lucia Harrison sipped her lemon water delicately. "By meeting her on that common ground you spoke of." She gave him a sly smile. "The way to a man is through his stomach, but the way to a woman is through the heart. You must become a part of something she loves."

Antony stared at his mother, ticking his head to the side. "You are far sneakier than I would have ever expected."

Her grin widened. "I believe the word you are looking for is shrewd." She shrugged. "I never sneak."

Antony laughed and shook his head. "I'll be sure and take your suggestion into consideration."

"You'll do it," she said firmly.

He smiled and sighed. "I'll do it."

At her nod of approval, they looked at the menus and went about their lunch.

An hour later, when he dropped her off at the mansion, his mother paused before getting out.

"Need to say something, Mother?" he asked, resting his arms on the steering wheel.

She tapped her fingers against her knee. "I was simply thinking of your father." She looked down at her fingers, admiring the ring on her right middle finger. It was a gift from her husband.

Antony's shoulders slumped. "I miss him too," he said quietly.

She nodded, then turned misty eyes in his direction. "If you think this woman has the possibility of being important to you, then do not waste time, Antony. Life can be far too precious."

Antony gave her a grim smile and stepped out of the vehicle. Walking around, he helped his mother to stand from her seat and gave her a hug. "I love you," he said.

She sniffled and returned his embrace, then stepped back and fluffed her hair. "Do not be dramatic," she snipped.

Antony chuckled at the irony in her statement. If there was one thing his mother was, it was dramatic. But he loved her for it. He turned to walk her up the steps, but she waved him off.

"Go. Take care of your bakery so you can work on winning a heart instead of a cookie" —she waved her hand— "thing."

"It's a gingerbread competition, Mother," he corrected, but smiled. "And I'll go, but I'll take you to dinner in a few days, yes?'

She nodded and headed inside.

His mind swirling with possibilities, ideas, and gratitude for his family, he gave the mansion a longing look, then got in his car and left. There would be time yet to see if Emory was willing to open her heart. First he had a business to run. Then he would figure out how to get himself into her kitchen for a little one-on-one time.

CHAPTER 3

It was several days before Emory saw Antony again, and in that time she had calmed down about the nougat, but other things had only become more difficult in other areas. Two days ago a pie had gone missing from the kitchen. First the nougat, now a pie. Emory was starting to think that someone was trying to sabotage her, or run her out of the kitchen. But who, and more importantly...why?

She and Bella had found the wrapper to the nougat on the back lawn of the property, and although it had frustrated Emory that someone had eaten it, she knew that there was no way it was Antony. He hadn't been at the mansion for either incident, unless he was sneaking around in the middle of the night like Hope had suggested, which simply didn't make sense. And with his type of talent, there was no reason why he should feel the need to sabotage Emory.

I think I knew that from the start, but I was too angry to see it, she chided herself mentally as she glued a piece of candy to her the roofline of her gingerbread house. She stepped back to admire her handiwork. The royal icing was setting nicely and she was pleased with how it was turning out. She had decided to build a replica of the mansion, with a few added details, for her entry into the gingerbread competition.

With a nickname like "Gingerbread Inn", Emory had decided to play up that name and give the mansion a little more whimsical flourish. The windows had already been done with isomalt and had set up as well as Emory could have asked them to. She had worked hard to make sure they looked frosted and wintery, and it had worked. Emory was currently working on the roof, and was completely dreading what was coming next.

Decorating was fine. She had a steady hand and was able to do lattice work like nobody's business, but putting the walls together? She always hated that part. As steady as she was with her piping, she shook like crazy when she was trying to put all the angles together.

A knock on her kitchen door had Emory pausing to turn around. "Yes?"

A dark head popped through the door. "Good evening, Emory."

Emory's heart skipped a beat at the divine grin aimed directly at her. He finished coming inside and began to saunter toward her. "What are you doing here?" she croaked, then hurriedly cleared her throat.

"What? No hello?" Antony put his hand over his heart as he stopped just a few feet in front of her.

Emory held back an eye roll. "I'm sorry." She mimicked his stance. "Oh, Antony!" she drawled in a high voice. "Whatever brings you to my kitchen tonight?"

His low, sultry chuckle sent goosebumps skittering down her spine. It really was a wonderful sound, much to Emory's dismay.

He stuffed his hands in his pockets and rocked back and forth on his heels. "As amusing as that was, I am very grateful you don't really sound like that."

Emory couldn't help but smile. "Me too," she admitted. "But you still haven't answered my question."

His grin grew. "I just dropped my mother off."

"Ah." Emory nodded. Her kitchen was suddenly feeling very warm. All it had taken was for Antony Harrison to step in and the temperature automatically spiked. Emory was equal parts frustrated and impressed. *So he's good-looking,* she scolded herself. *Why do I have to be so affected by it?* The back part of her brain answered. *Because he's also intriguing and an excellent baker. Who wouldn't be affected by that?*

His face grew serious. "I wanted to ask about your nougat," he said, his voice dropping. "Did you ever find it?'

Shame sunk into Emory's chest and felt like a two-ton weight. She dropped her gaze to the ground, unable to look him in the eye after being reminded of her horrible behavior. "Yeah...about that." She swallowed hard, her eyes on her apron. She smudged a line of food coloring. "I, uh, found the wrapper." She glanced up from under her eyelashes.

Antony's dark brows were high on his forehead, making his gray eyes look wide. "Someone ate it? What did they do? Leave the garbage lying around?"

She shrugged. "It would appear so."

"Wow." Antony shook his head. "That's horrible." He snorted. "I'll bet they didn't even bother to savor it."

"Speaking of which," Emory forced herself to say. "I need to apologize."

A slow grin grew on Antony's face. "Do you?" He stepped a little closer.

Emory felt her cheeks flush. No matter how smirky he got, she knew how to admit she was wrong. *Mostly.* "Yes." She straightened her shoulders. "I'm sorry for accusing you of stealing, especially since I had no evidence. I was frustrated and angry and took it out on the first viable target."

The mischief in Antony's eyes was practically glowing. "That was a very clean apology. Well done."

She nodded, then waited. And waited. "Aren't you going to say anything?"

He shrugged. "I don't know. I'm not sure whether or not I should forgive you. After all...my reputation was horribly damaged from your accusations."

Oh, brother. "It was, huh?"

"Definitely." He stepped even closer.

Emory had to tilt her head back to see him now. "I suppose you want me to do something to make it better?"

He gave her an innocent look. "It might help."

"What do you suggest?" she asked, working to keep her voice nonchalant. His nearness was messing with her head. He smelled like his bakery and at the thought, Emory's mouth began to water. His pastries had been amazing, though she wasn't ready to admit that to him.

"My mother always said a kiss makes everything better," he ventured.

She glared, forcing back her excited hormones. "And mine said a cookie did, so..." Emory spun around, grabbed an extra shortbread cookie on her counter, then turned and held it out.

He looked at it, then looked at her. It was clear he wasn't impressed with her trade.

"Go on," Emory said, waving it closer to his nose. "Sugar always does a body good."

Without breaking eye contact, Antony opened his mouth and caught the cookie between his teeth, taking a large, slow bite.

Emory suddenly found her mouth very...very...dry. She swallowed hard, but it did no good. His intensity and seductive actions were more than she could handle. *I'm in wayyyyy over my head,* she thought miserably.

"Your cookie is just like I knew it would be," he murmured around his mouthful.

"What? Overdone?" she snapped, desperately trying to draw on any other emotion than desire.

He shook his head and leaned down until they were practically nose to nose. "Sweet and sandy, with just the right amount of salt."

Her breathing was so erratic that Emory was afraid for a moment that she was going to pass out. This guy was good. Too good. How in the world was she supposed to keep from falling for him? He was handsome, a marvelous baker, his voice could melt butter, and he obviously knew how to push her buttons.

How do I fight this? She had a momentary pause. *Do I want to fight this?*

ANTONY HELD VERY STILL. He could practically see the emotions running through Emory's brain and he was afraid if he broke her concentration, he would send her over the edge. When he'd dropped his mother off for the evening, he'd decided it was time to make a move.

It had been a couple of days since they'd seen each other, and he'd been gathering his courage along with learning as much as he could about her before striking again.

"Thank you," she whispered, her blue eyes wide and still undecided.

Antony straightened up and gave her a break from his assault. It was also a much needed break for himself. If he stayed close to the sweet-smelling baker much longer, he might take a bite of her instead of the cookie. *Speaking of which...* Antony reached out and took the cookie from her clammy fingers, stuffing the rest of it in his mouth. "I didn't have dessert after dinner," he said when he'd swallowed. "That was perfect. Not too sweet, not too savory."

"There was lavender in it," she said, still looking a little lost.

Antony smiled and nodded. "I could tell. I'll have to try that in my own sometime."

Emory cleared her throat and wiped her hands on her apron. "I'll, uh, get you the recipe."

"Or you could just show me," he said. "I always did learn a little better with hands-on instruction." He held back his laughter when all the blood drained from her face. Obviously, this woman was not used to someone flirting with her.

"I'm sure you already have a shortbread recipe."

"I do." He nodded. "But I like to expand my horizons." His eyes traveled to the table behind her. "Is that your gingerbread house?"

"Crap!" Emory interjected, spinning to the table, then back to him. Her uncertainty vanished and she became the spitfire he found intriguing. Stepping forward, she poked him in the chest. "You aren't supposed to see that. No one is supposed to see the other contestant's stuff before the day of the competition."

Antony crossed his heart and put his fingers in the air. "I promise not to use this against you." Then he stepped around her hand and walked up to the table. "Emory," he said breathlessly. "You are a true artist."

Her work was amazing. Her piping skills were some of the best he'd ever seen. It was amazing that she wasn't working in some high-end bakery in New York.

"I...thank you," she said, confusion in her tone. He'd apparently thrown her off with his compliment.

Antony shook his head. "I mean it. I can't do anything like this." He held up his hands. "These large hands don't do the tiny details." He grinned. "But I'm not too bad at carving and sculpture."

She tilted her head, considering him. "Were those pictures, on the walls of your bakery, your work?"

He beamed, completely flattered she had noticed. "They were."

Emory gave him a sheepish grin. "I guess we both have different strengths then, because it was incredible work."

The tension in the room shifted and it was a welcome change. Instead of fiery fireworks, it now felt more comfortable and welcoming, like a warm hearth. While the sparks were fun, Antony knew that putting her at ease was going to be the best way to get in her good graces. "Will you show me how you do it?" he asked.

She frowned. "What? The piping?"

He nodded eagerly. "I'd love to watch you work."

She hesitated.

"Please? You can consider this a technique lesson."

Emory laughed a little. "Does that mean I should charge you for my time?"

He shrugged. "If that makes you feel better."

LAURA ANN

Emory snorted. "That's all right. I don't mind." She walked past him and picked up the piping bag, only hesitating once more before she leaned over and began creating a lovely design on one of the building windows.

"You used isomalt?" he asked.

She nodded. "Yeah. I left it bubbly so it would look frosted."

He hummed his agreement. "It worked. Especially with your designs, the whole thing screams winter wonderland." He watched her small, thin hands move in short, smooth strokes, leaving behind an intricate weaving that added the perfect ambiance to the home. "I could sit and watch you all day," he murmured, before he could think better of it.

She halted, the piping bag slowly dropping. "I don't know what to do when you say things like that," she whispered.

Antony drew closer. "Why do anything at all?" He could see her breathing pick up, and the indecision came back into her eyes. He broke their staredown and looked back at the gingerbread house. "It looks like you're almost ready to assemble."

She nodded, taking a minute to answer him. "Yeah...I'm trying not to worry about that part."

He frowned. "Why? Aren't you excited to see it all together?"

She shrugged. "Yeah, but I always struggle with the building part. I seem to be more of a decorator."

"Would you like some help?" he automatically asked. She had left the perfect opening for him to spend more time with her and he was going to take shameless advantage.

Her frown grew and she scrunched up her nose. "Uh...no thanks. I can do it."

Antony chuckled. "I realize we didn't really get off on the right foot. Can we try again?" He straightened and folded his arms over his chest. "I won't mince words, Emory. I've never been good at subterfuge. I'm attracted to you." He held up a hand to stop her response. "I know

I was teasing you about it the other day, but I think you're interested as well." He raised an eyebrow, daring her to disagree.

Emory sighed and dropped the piping tube, then rubbed her temples. "I'm so confused."

Antony couldn't help it. He reached out and rubbed the back of her neck. It was a friendly, but still slightly intimate move that allowed him to touch her without coming on too strong. "Does your head hurt?"

"My brain hurts," she admitted, then sighed and dropped her head forward. "That feels way better than it should."

The door to the kitchen banged open, cutting off Antony's response.

"Emory!" Bella shouted, then skidded to a stop with her mouth open. Emory squeaked and jumped away from Antony's touch.

He grit his teeth, frustrated to have his moment interrupted, but accepting there was nothing he could do about it.

"Well, isn't this fortuitous," Bella said with a smirk. She folded her arms and cocked her hip. "I was just coming to get your phone number," she said to Antony.

He raised his eyebrows.

"Your mother lost a ring and she's about to take Hope out in an epic WWE showdown."

Emory gasped as Antony used his long legs to quickly lead himself out of the kitchen and toward the screeching he could now hear that was most definitely his mother. *Ironic that she's the one who pushed me to pursue Emory, only to be the reason my efforts are thwarted.* He shook his head. "This better be good."

CHAPTER 4

E mory followed Antony out of the kitchen, ignoring Bella's knowing look as they headed to the front of the mansion. She was still
shaken from the incident in the kitchen. His hands had been warm and
felt so good against her tight muscles. The stress of trying to upkeep
Grandma's legacy and take care of the bed and breakfast had been overwhelming, but Emory was fighting with all she had.

That, however, had led to sleepless nights and sore muscles. *I need
a good yoga session,* she lamented. But there was no time for that now.
Right now her cousin was being accused of stealing, something Emory
had accused Antony of only a few days previous. "Who the heck would
think Bella could steal anything?" she muttered.

"Someone not thinking clearly," Bella answered drily.

Emory snapped her mouth shut. She hadn't meant to speak her
thoughts out loud and right now was not the time to get in a conversation with Bella. Her journalist cousin would interrogate Emory until
she had every detail of what had occurred in the kitchen.

"Mother?" Antony called out as they arrived in the foyer.

"Antony!" Mrs. Harrison cried. "They have taken my ring! It is
gone!"

Emory stayed in the entrance, watching Antony hug his mother
and work to calm her down.

"It's going to be okay, Mom. Just take a deep breath and we'll get it
all figured out."

"It's gone," she wailed. "Goooone!"

Antony nodded again. "I know, Mom. We'll figure it out. It's okay."
He began leading her away from the foyer, walking past Emory to go
into the large sitting room. "Let's sit down and we'll call the police and

get it all taken care of." He glanced over his shoulder to Bella and raised his eyebrows.

"On it," she said quickly, rushing to the front desk phone.

Emory slowly followed Antony, though she still stayed in the background. His mother was nearly inconsolable, but Emory was struggling with her own emotions. Antony was being so sweet. Nothing like the arrogant man he liked to play when he and she were together.

Emory glanced over her shoulder, suddenly remembering Hope, but Enoch, who had been spending a lot of time with Hope, was taking care of her cousin, so Emory put her attention back on the proceedings in the sitting room.

Grandma Claire came shuffling in. "Mrs. Harrison?"

The woman looked up from where she sat.

"I understand we've had a robbery," Grandma Claire said softly, settling herself in a nearby chair. She shook her head. "I'm so sorry. Bella has called the police and we'll get to the bottom of this."

Mrs. Harrison straightened her back. "The only person who has been in my room is your granddaughter, the housekeeper. She is the one who has done this."

Emory pinched her lips. She'd given into her own emotions not long ago and said some things she didn't mean, so she tried to be charitable to Mrs. Harrison, but Hope wouldn't snitch a piece of cookie dough, let alone a ring.

Grandma Claire smiled gently. "While I'm terribly sorry about what has happened to you, I can assure you Hope had nothing to do with it. My granddaughter is completely trustworthy."

Emory looked over as Hope came in, holding tightly onto Enoch. *Those two have grown really close,* Emory mused. She looked at their combined fingers and couldn't help but smile. *Looks like Hope might not be leaving after Christmas after all.*

Murmured voices were the only sound in the room for several minutes before a noise in the front entry caught everyone's attention.

"Claire?"

Everyone turned to see Sheriff Davidson storming into the room. The first thing he did was head straight to Grandma. Emory covered her grin with her fingers. Between Hope and Enoch and Grandma and Sheriff Davidson, there was much more than Christmas carols in the air. Though Emory had noticed that the sheriff and her grandmother did little more than eye one another from afar.

"What's this about another theft?" the sheriff asked.

"Another?" cried Mrs. Harrison. She squished up her face. "What type of place have you put me, Antony? A place where they steal things willy nilly? Have you no more care for me than that?"

"Mother, stop," Antony said firmly. "You knew about the missing candy. You were there when Emory accused me."

Mrs. Harrison sniffed. "As if you would do such a thing."

"I could say the same thing about Hope," Bella shot out.

"Bella," Grandma Claire responded, "a little decorum, please."

Bella gave Mrs. Harrison a defiant look. "I'm not worried about being in your good graces, nor am I too soft-spoken to fight back," she stated when Mrs. Harrison glared. "You came downstairs and threw out accusations like they were nothing when you have no real evidence."

"I do have evidence!" Mrs. Harrison argued.

"Then I, for one, would like to hear it," Sheriff Davidson said. He walked over to a chair and plopped down before removing his hat. "Excuse me, Claire," he said sheepishly. "I should have taken it off at the door."

Grandma Claire nodded. "Nothing to worry about, William. I just want this solved."

As if they had a tangible connection, Emory felt Antony's eyes latch onto her and she couldn't help but look back. He gave her an apologetic smile and Emory nodded. While she didn't like her cousin being treated unfairly, Emory could hardly be upset when she'd done the same thing.

They spent the next half-hour hashing out all the problems that had been occurring around the mansion, from stolen goods to doors being mysteriously left open, and Enoch had even spotted an intruder prowling the grounds one evening.

Emory shivered. It was all getting way too creepy around here. Her load was heavy enough. She didn't need to add criminal activity to the list.

After declaring that he was going to call in a favor with a detective friend, Sheriff Davidson stood. "I guess I'll be on my way, then," he said, working his way to the front door.

"Here, Sheriff," Emory said, stalling his progress. She rushed to the kitchen and wrapped a croissant in a napkin before coming back out and handing it to him. "Something for the road."

The sheriff smiled and tipped his head. "Thank you, Ms. Emory. I sure do love your cooking."

Emory couldn't help but smile. "You're welcome. And I love anyone who loves my baking, so I guess it all works out."

The sheriff chuckled, tipped his hat to the rest of the room, and left.

Grandma wasted no time in climbing to her feet and inviting Mrs. Harrison to take a walk with her. After a bit of initial arguing, the two women headed out into the cool, winter air.

AS THE ROOM BEGAN TO calm down, Antony walked slowly toward Emory. He wasn't sure how she would receive him after the drama of the last half-hour. "She's not so bad when you get to know her," he said softly, hoping the apology in his voice was clear.

She nodded quickly and played with the ends of her apron strings. "I'm sure you're right."

"That ring was my father's last gift to her before he passed," he continued.

Emory's eyebrows drooped at the sides. "I'm so sorry. No wonder she's devastated."

Antony nodded slowly. "Thank you." He looked around and felt even more uncomfortable when he found they had a rapt audience. Clearing his throat, he jabbed his thumb toward the front entrance. "I guess I better be going, then, huh?"

"Uh, yeah. Thanks for coming to...help," Emory stammered. Her body language said she was just as uncomfortable as he was.

He pinched his lips together. "I'm sorry for her outburst. I'm sure we'll get it all figured out." Without waiting for another answer, he made a beeline for the front door, rushing out before he could be stopped.

Once outside, he took a couple of deep breaths. "Shoot," he muttered as he made his way to his car. He hadn't been ready to leave quite yet, but the circumstances had seemed to dictate it.

He slid behind the driver's seat and thumped the steering wheel with his thumbs. The feeling persisted. He simply didn't want to go yet. "But how can I go back in there with everything that just happened?"

Before he could come up with an answer, another car pulled into the driveway. Antony watched an older woman get out of her vehicle and march her way up the stairs. He snickered a little at the proud tilt of her head. "She's not going to be an easy guest." Then he immediately frowned. "Where's her luggage?"

Bella had already let the woman inside, but Antony's curiosity was piqued. Before he could think too much about it, he got out of his car and hurried to the back of the mansion. If he wasn't mistaken, there had been an outside door in the kitchen. He eyed the wall of the building until he felt like he was at approximately the right spot and sure enough, there was a screened door with two small steps.

Antony knocked, then blew on his hands and rubbed them together. The wind outside was bitterly cold and he had a momentary flash of worry for his mother, but it melted like glazed icing on a hot cake when Emory opened the door.

"Antony!" she said in surprise. "What are you doing?"

"At the moment, I'm trying to get warm," he joked.

"Oh my gosh. Come in," Emory said, opening the screen door and ushering him inside. After the doors were closed, Antony took a deep breath and sighed. The heat of the kitchen was not only familiar, but felt perfect against his cold skin. "Now." Emory tapped her foot. "An explanation, please."

He grinned at her impatience. She was a mover and a shaker, that was for sure. "I, uh...well..." He scrunched up his nose. "This is going to sound slightly stalkerish, but I watched a woman come to the front door before I left and she didn't have any luggage on her. I was curious." He shrugged, feeling like an idiot, but unable to do anything about it at the moment.

Emory rubbed her temple. "I suppose anyone would be after everything that's been happening around here."

He nodded a little too quickly, grateful she had given him a clean excuse.

"But I don't know who the woman was," Emory continued. "Bella deals with the guests."

"Emory?" Bella asked from the doorway. Her mouth pulled into an excited smile when she spotted Antony. "Well, well, well...Antony, I suppose this would involve you as well, so you might as well come on out."

Antony looked to Emory, who shook her head with wide eyes to indicate she had no idea what was going on. "Okay," she said hesitantly, turning back to Bella. "We're coming."

Antony followed her out of the kitchen, to find the woman waiting with her arms folded over her ample chest. Recognition hit Antony like a meat hammer and he had to hold in a groan. "Mrs. Pearson," he said, forcing a polite tone to his voice. From behind and with that hat over her face, he hadn't known who it was. If he had, he would have told Emory to come outside, rather than come inside himself.

Mrs. Pearson tsked her tongue. "It's you."

"Yes, it is." Antony slipped into the charming persona he put on with irate customers. "I had no idea I'd have the pleasure of seeing you today."

"I'm sure you didn't," she snapped. "But I'm not here to see you." Her dark eyes snapped to Emory. "I'm here to see the room the competition is going to be in and make sure it's up to snuff this year. Heaven knows your grandmother could barely keep it tolerable in there. The light was never good enough." She sniffed. "And now she's handed it over to you." Mrs. Pearson eyed Emory from top to bottom and Antony found himself taking a step forward.

Something protective rose up inside of him and he felt anger on Emory's behalf from the treatment of this woman. Mrs. Pearson had come in second place several years in the competition and she had made it known to the whole town that this year she refused to take home the number two ribbon again.

People might care if she was nice enough to care about, Antony thought. He proceeded to scold himself for his unkindness, but it was hard to stop the thoughts. Betty Pearson was a nosy old biddy who made it her business to tell everyone else your business. And if the information was bad or unfounded, she loved it all the more.

There's at least one in every town, he reminded himself. *But that doesn't mean Emory has to deal with it.*

He opened his mouth to snap something back, but Emory spoke up.

"Actually, Mrs. Pearson, the room isn't quite done yet." She smiled sweetly and clasped her hands in front of herself. "I'd be happy to show you what we've done if you'd like a sneak peek."

Mrs. Pearson sniffed and then wrinkled her nose as if she smelled something spoiled. "Might as well. That way I can fix it if you've ruined it worse than Claire did."

Antony watched Emory lead the ornery woman away while he stood next to Bella, whose jaw was nearly on the floor.

"I think someone needs to give that lady a taste of her own medicine," Bella whispered.

Antony nodded. "She's definitely not the person you want to meet in a dark alley."

Bella snorted, then turned to give him a considering look. "I thought you left."

Antony felt heat crawl up his neck. "You know...I don't think Emory should be left alone with her. Who knows what'll happen." He smiled when Bella laughed at his abrupt departure, but what was he supposed to say? That he was so intrigued by Emory that he wanted more time with her? That he'd pulled out a lame excuse just to see her for a few more minutes? That he couldn't seem to stop himself from wondering if she tasted like the cookies she baked?

Antony shook his head. "Stay the course," he told himself. "This one is going to have to be slow and steady. Emory is definitely not the kind to leap before she looks."

As frustrating as that was, the challenge of it was still extremely appealing. So, putting on his best smile, he came up behind the women and kept it plastered in place as he listened to Mrs. Pearson provide a commentary on everything that was wrong with the room.

CHAPTER 5

Emory whacked the dough in front of her, picturing Mrs. Pearson's face. "Take that," she muttered under her breath, then sighed. "So violent." She shook her head at her own ridiculousness. Glancing up at the wall, she balked when she realized what time it was. The detective was going to be here in just a few minutes and she was covered in flour.

Whipping off her apron and straightening her hair, she headed to the sitting room, then skidded to a halt when she realized no one was there. "Where are they?" she grumbled, heading to the front entryway.

She discovered Hope cleaning and together, they gathered almost everyone who needed to be present. Emory found herself constantly looking toward the front door and it drove her crazy. *Stop watching for him!* But she couldn't seem to help herself. Somehow during the couple of weeks Emory had been in Seagull Cove, Antony had gone from being an extreme irritant to something...interesting.

His handsome looks had always been intriguing, but it was more than that pulling her in now. It was his smooth voice, his laughter, and the way he cared for his mother. He'd admitted he wanted to get to know her and had said she was attractive. She couldn't help but admire a man who wasn't afraid to admit those things.

But Emory also found herself drawn to the fact that they both baked, and Antony's skills were divine. And most of all, he seemed genuinely concerned about her. He had wanted to make her head feel better. He'd tried to intervene when Mrs. Pearson had come in and thrown around insults like they were chopped nuts on top of a cake. He'd asked about her work and seemed eager to learn her technique secrets.

Is he just trying to hedge his bets for the gingerbread competition? Or is he serious in his interest? Does he really find me attractive?

The opening of the front door had Emory straightening up. Her eyes happened to catch those of Mrs. Harrison and Emory offered a small, unsure smile and wave. The woman was completely intimidating. Antony treated her like a precious doll, but Emory could only see hardness. She cleared her throat when Mrs. Harrison didn't return the sentiment and looked away.

"Hello, Mother," Antony said, going immediately to Mrs. Harrison's side. After kissing her cheek, he looked around the room until his eyes caught with Emory's. He smiled widely at her and walked her way. "How are you today?" he asked softly.

Emory nodded politely. "Doing all right. You?"

He shrugged. "I think my bakery assistant is tired of all the time I'm spending away from the kitchen, but fine."

Emory frowned. "Is your business going to be okay? You've spent a lot of time out here lately."

Antony chuckled and reached out to run a finger down her cheek. "Are you concerned for me, Emory?"

His touch ignited a flame in her belly and Emory sucked in a breath. "I..I just don't want you to lose business because something weird is happening out here at the inn."

He shook his head. "Don't worry. I do most of my work before the world rises." His grin widened. "You should understand that."

She nodded, all too understanding. "Yeah...I get it. College was rough with that schedule. I never got to experience the nightlife all the other students enjoyed."

Antony shrugged. "It's not that great."

Emory's eyebrows shot up. "Are you telling me you stayed up late?"

He nodded. "I didn't go to culinary school, so I didn't experience the lifestyle."

Her jaw slackened. "Wait...what? But the sculptures...the awards..."

He shrugged again, then stuffed his hands in his pockets. "My mother is Italian, if you couldn't tell by the accent." He let his accent come forward more and Emory nodded.

As if he isn't swoony enough, she thought.

"The recipes I use are things that have been passed down for generations." He nodded toward his mother, who was now speaking with Grandma Claire. "She taught me everything I know." He snorted. "Well, that and Food Network."

"Holy cow…Antony, that's…amazing," Emory said. She couldn't imagine trying to make it in this business with nothing but time spent with her mother. "What did you study originally?"

He kept a very straight face and said, "Accounting."

Emory pinched her lips together. "You can't be serious." Her body shook slightly as she tried to hold in her laughter. The thought of Antony behind a desk, schmoozing people while he did their taxes, did not work for her.

He burst out laughing. "No. I studied art."

A light bulb went off. "Your sculptures!"

He nodded. "Yeah. Sculpting was my thing, but I couldn't shake the need to be in the kitchen."

"So you combined them," she finished.

Antony nodded, looking sheepish.

"Why are you embarrassed?" Emory pressed. "That's absolutely incredible."

He rubbed the back of his neck. "I don't know. Telling women you were an artist always sounds…weird."

"Unless that woman is into art," Emory pointed out before she could think better of it.

His eyes lit up with that glow that spoke of passion and fun. "And are you one of those women, Emory?" He stepped a little closer.

"Maybe," she managed to squeak.

Before he could speak any more, Hope walked in with the detective. His square jaw gave him a rugged handsomeness that Emory couldn't help but notice. "Detective, this is my cousin, Emory."

He nodded. "Miss."

Emory smiled. "Welcome. Can I get you a donut? I made some fresh this morning."

"I suppose I'm talking to the baker, then," he said with a grin.

Emory's smile widened. "Correct."

"In that case, I'd be a fool to turn down anything you made. Bill says your cooking comes straight from heaven."

Emory's cheeks pinked up and she nearly jumped when a hand landed on her lower back.

"ANTONY HARRISON," ANTONY stated firmly, leaning forward to shake hands. "Also a baker." He didn't like the way this guy had lit up at Emory's name. Antony might not have any real hold on Emory, but he was trying, and wasn't about to let a new guy get in the way.

Detective Gordon responded in kind. "Nice to meet you. It's your mom who's missing the ring, correct?"

Antony nodded toward his mother. "That is my mother, Lucia Harrison."

"Ma'am," the detective said. "Don't worry. We'll find your jewelry."

Mrs. Harrison sniffed. "I hope so."

"This is my grandmother, Claire Simmons," Hope continued. She looked around. "Where's Bella?"

"Coming!" Bella bounded into the room, her strawberry blonde hair blowing behind her. "Whew! I made it." She skidded to a stop, her mouth gaping as she looked at Detective Gordon. Her open mouth snapped into a wide smile. "Well, hello..."

Antony choked a little at her boldness. When Emory frowned and began to pound on his back, it only made him laugh more. He grabbed her hand and gave it a squeeze. "Thanks," he whispered hoarsely.

She glared. "That wasn't funny."

Antony pinched his fingers together. "It was a little bit." Using her hand to tug her forward, he took the opportunity to whisper in her ear. "And Enoch thought so too." He pointed to where the handyman was turning bright red and trying to hide his laughter behind his fist.

Emory rolled her eyes, but didn't move away.

Ha! Progress!

"You must be Isabella," Detective Gordon said smoothly, his eyes focused on the new arrival..

"I must be, indeed," she said, sashaying further into the room. "And you are?"

"Detective Gordon." He smiled. "Henry Gordon. But everyone calls me Hank."

"Nice to meet you, Hank."

Antony nearly lost it again. Only Emory's fierce look made him swallow his amusement. Instead, he cleared his throat and casually let their entwined hands hang between them. He wasn't sure if she even remembered he was holding onto her, but he wasn't going to let go until he had to.

As the rest of the group began to tell the detective everything that had been happening around the inn, Antony turned his attention back to Emory. "Has anything else weird happened since I was here last?"

She sighed and rubbed her temple with her free hand. "Yeah."

Antony frowned. "What?'

She scrunched her nose and peered up at him. "A pie went missing."

"What?" he said a little too loudly, then ducked when a few heads turned his way. "What do you mean a pie went missing?"

She gave him a wry look. "Exactly what I said. The other day I made six pies. After I left for awhile, there were only five when I came back."

Antony shook his head. "That is so strange. Do you think it's the same person who took the ring?"

Emory shrugged. "No idea. The two don't seem like they should be related, do they?"

He shook his head, agreeing with her. "No. One seems like someone who's hungry. The other is a real crime."

She narrowed her gaze. "Stealing one of my pies *is* a real crime."

He grinned. "I'm sure it is. I have absolutely no doubt that a pie made by you is worth stealing." He leaned in a little. "As a side note...how come you didn't offer me a donut?"

Emory slipped her hand from his and crossed her arms over her chest. "I was trying to be polite."

Antony nodded slowly. "I see. This wouldn't have anything to do with him being good-looking, would it?"

Emory choked on a laugh. "What? Is the egomaniac worried about a little competition?"

Antony studied his fingernails, trying to appear unaffected. "No. But maybe I'm feeling left out. Especially after I offered you some of my goods the other day."

Emory laughed lightly. "I don't think I ever thanked you for those. They were totally worth the extra workout I had to do."

A wide smile spread across his face. "Desserts are always worth it."

She nodded and her smile turned shy, before she dropped his gaze. "If you want a donut...or two, you're welcome to them. I made apple cider donuts for breakfast. A couple of seconds in the microwave and they should be as good as new."

"As soon as...Hank is gone. I think I'll take you up on that," Antony said easily. He paused. "But seriously...did you find him attractive?"

Emory's mouth twitched as she turned his way. "You really are worried."

Antony looked away, embarrassed, but wanting to know the truth. While he didn't mind standing up to another man for Emory's attention, he wasn't going to fight if she wasn't interested.

Emory's hand on his arm grabbed his attention. "First of all," she said softly, "I have no intention of fighting against my cousin." She tilted her head and smirked. "And I think she's already called dibs." Emory put up her hand to stop his next question. "But even if she hadn't, I wouldn't be interested."

Slowly, Antony put his hand over hers, keeping them connected. "Is there anyone you would be interested in?"

She chewed her lip for a moment, only heightening Antony's anxiety. "Quite possibly," she finally answered. "But I shouldn't be."

"Why not?"

"Because he's my competitor."

Antony pulled her hand off his arm and settled it into his other hand, twining their fingers once more. "A little healthy competition never hurt anybody," he answered. "Besides, we both know I'm going to win anyway, so there really isn't a competition." He chuckled when she slugged his shoulder.

"Not to mention he's got an ego the size of Alaska."

"Emory?"

"Hmm?"

"Would you be willing to bake with me?"

She looked surprised by his request. "Uh..."

Antony reached out and tucked a stray hair behind her ear. "I thoroughly enjoyed our few minutes in your kitchen the other day. Would you be willing to bake and decorate some cookies with me?"

She gave a breathy laugh. "Is that your way of asking me on a date?"

He shrugged. "Sort of. Mostly I just want to spend time with you. And if it includes sweet treats, then all the better."

Her cheeks were slightly pink as she thought on his answer. "I think that sounds like fun," she finally responded.

Antony nodded. "Let me look at my schedule and we'll get it figured out."

Both of them went silent as they turned back to the busy conversation with the detective. *Hopefully we'll get the mysteries settled quickly, so that I can have Emory's attention to myself,* Antony thought. *But for now...I'll take what I can get.*

CHAPTER 6

Are you going to let me in?

Emory frowned at her phone, then looked around the kitchen. "Let him in?" She had just delivered a tray of snacks and drinks to Bella and Detective Gordon, who were sitting in the dining room, getting cozy, and now Antony was asking to be let in. "He must be at the front door and Bella's not there," Emory murmured to herself and began to walk out of the kitchen. A knock stopped her movement.

Turning, she walked to the back door of the kitchen and opened it wide. She smirked. "So is this your new permanent entrance?"

Antony shrugged one shoulder. "I don't mind the idea of a personal entrance."

Emory rolled her eyes. "Of course you wouldn't." She stepped back and let him in. "Geez, it's cold," she whined as she shut the door behind him.

"Missing Seattle?"

Emory paused. She hated to say it, but she wasn't. Her boss was a difficult man to get along with, the weather was always wet, and she never got credit for anything she did. Even with all the stress of her situation, coming to Seagull Cove might have been the best thing that could have happened to her. "Doesn't everyone miss their home?" she asked, not ready to admit her feelings to him. "It's not quite as cold as here."

Antony had set his coat on the back of a chair and was rubbing his hands together. "Yeah…it's not the best weather, but I've dealt with much worse, that's for sure."

Emory hummed her agreement and went back to her work. Antony's presence always set her nerves on edge. Her hands shook and her heart raced. She was actually struggling to remember what she had been doing before he'd randomly shown up, though she wasn't upset at his coming. More and more she found herself wanting to spend time with him, but not wanting to admit it. He was a distraction. A handsome distraction, but a distraction nonetheless.

"How has your morning been?" he asked, settling into a bar stool, looking completely at ease.

She shrugged. "Fine. Uneventful." A loud thump from over their heads caught their attention and they both looked up.

"Do you guys have a cat?" Antony asked with a grin.

A loud crash was followed by several screams. "That would be one heck of a cat," Emory muttered before hurrying to get out of the kitchen.

"Hold up!" Antony called, coming in right behind her.

Emory skidded to a stop at the bottom of the stairs. Detective Hank and Bella were at a door on the landing, and the crying and screaming was a little bit frightening.

Antony put a hand on her lower back. "Should we check it out?"

Emory swallowed hard and looked across the foyer to see Grandma Claire coming.

"What in the world is going on?" she asked, walking as quickly as she could.

"I don't know," Emory admitted. Her eyes drifted to the open doorway again.

"Well, then, let's go," Grandma snapped.

Emory was grateful when Antony took her grandmother's elbow and began to help her up the stairs. By the time they got there, the detective was dragging a bedraggled woman out of the room. Emory frowned, realizing it was the woman she'd met at the candy store in town. *What was her name?* She wracked her brain, but ended up distracted when she peered inside the guest suite. Hope was sitting on

Enoch's lap, looking like she was in shell shock. Her cheek was bleeding and Emory gasped, taking a step forward.

"Hold on," Antony said softly. "From the way she's gripping Enoch, I think we better leave her be."

Emory's hands were shaking fiercely, but she fished her phone out of her pocket and dialed 911, asking for an ambulance. Once done, she put her phone away. "Emergency people are on their way," she said, and Antony nodded. "That cheek definitely needs to be looked at."

Antony let out a long breath. "I wonder what exactly happened here."

Emory shook her head. "I don't know, but it definitely wasn't good."

Thirty minutes later, the crowd had gone home and Hope and Enoch had headed in for stitches, leaving Emory alone in her kitchen. Normally being alone was her favorite way to be, but tonight, the silence felt oppressive.

The weight of the arrest sat heavily on her shoulders. Emory had realized later that the woman's name was Trisha, and apparently she had been a friend of Enoch's, not to mention a worker at the inn previous to its shutdown. *But why would she hurt Hope, and what caused her to be so desperate she needed to steal?*

Her pocket buzzed and she checked her phone, desperate for some information.

Come bake cookies with me tonight.

Emory bit her lip. She wasn't sure her head was in the right place for a date, but considering all that had happened, a distraction wasn't completely unwelcome. Taking a deep breath, she decided it was a good time to stretch her wings a bit, and if Antony's strong arms were involved, it might not be such a bad situation.

Okay.

She arrived that evening just as the clerk was locking up.

"Oh, hey!" Jennifer said with a cheery wave. "Mr. Harrison said to let you through." Jennifer relocked things and then headed toward the back. "He's this way."

Emory felt particularly awkward having the teenage girl there. Here Emory was, meeting the boss for a sort-of-date, and the employee was showing her around. But she dutifully followed Jennifer to the back. Once she was through the door, Emory found herself stopping and taking in the ambiance.

Cinnamon, sugar, browned butter...it all floated through the air as a permanent air freshener. Stainless steel ovens, stoves, counters, and fridges were laid out in an efficient way that Emory could certainly appreciate.

Considering that Antony's bakery was fairly new, she understood that this had to be the result of a massive renovation and she had to admit he did a good job.

"He's around here somewhere," Jennifer murmured, standing on her tiptoes and looking around the space.

"It's okay," Emory assured Jennifer. "I'll find him."

She smiled. "Okey, doke. I'll head out and leave you to it." With a cute wave, the worker was gone.

Emory sighed and began to look around, taking in more of the details. Just as he had out front, Antony had put up large posters of chocolate sculptures and even some that didn't look like food. One in particular caught Emory's eye and she walked over to look at it closely. The art was a sculpture of a Christmas elf and Emory was floored by the amount of detail and how little he looked like cake.

Only a couple of tells were visible to her that let her know the confection was edible. She shook her head. "Wow. Oh!" She jumped when a warm presence came up behind her and kissed her cheek.

"You made it," Antony said softly in her ear.

Laughing awkwardly, Emory turned to look at him, stepping into the wall when she discovered he was so close. He smelled like vanilla and his hair was a mess, but he looked utterly scrumptious. "I did," she said breathlessly.

His eyes were twinkling with that familiar mischief and Emory, the avid rule follower, found herself wanting to fall into them and never come up for air. There was something so inviting about a man who enjoyed life with gusto. Emory had spent much of her adulthood with her nose to the grindstone, and Antony seemed to be the complete opposite. A love of food tied them together, but otherwise, he intimidated her with his carefree, over-confident way of tackling life.

"I grabbed some take-out, so I didn't fill you with only sugar." He smirked and ran his knuckle along her jawline. "You strike me as the type who always eats their vegetables first."

Emory laughed lightly and nodded. "I hate to admit it, but yeah...I am."

He reached out and took her hand in his. "Then come, Em. Let me feed you."

She lost her breath at his words and nickname. There was something purely seductive about the way he'd said those innocent words, and Emory felt completely helpless to resist him.

ANTONY'S HEART WAS close to beating out of his chest. He hadn't been this nervous for a date in...ever. Having never lacked in confidence, Antony had never found himself worrying about whether or not a woman would enjoy what he had planned. *And yet here we are. I'm sweating about making cookies. How stupid is that?*

"Do you like pasta?"

Emory laughed. "An Italian man feeding me pasta. That sounds like a romance movie."

He smirked. "I won't turn that description down."

Emory's face turned red and she dropped his gaze. It was adorable to him. He loved that she wasn't just accepting of compliments as if she deserved or received them all the time. Her shyness only made him want to push more and watch her reaction.

He tugged her over to a small table he'd set up in the back of the kitchen. While a business kitchen wasn't the most romantic place, he'd set up a couple of candles and tried to separate the area from the work zone as much as he could.

"Wow," Emory said. "You really went all out."

"Doesn't every man who wants to impress a woman?" He pulled out her chair.

"You want to impress me?" she whispered.

Antony paused and made sure he was looking her in the eye. "Is it working?"

"A little too well," she admitted, then swallowed hard.

The urge to kiss those pink lips was overwhelming, but Antony kept himself in check. He absolutely planned to kiss her, but if he started that now, he was afraid nothing else would get done, and he had a fun evening planned. *Take the time to warm her up first,* he reminded himself. *She deserves that much.*

After a short grace, they dug in.

"Mmm..." Emory said, closing her eyes as she chewed her bolognese. "This is delicious. Who made it?"

Antony poked at his plate. "Would you freak out if I said my mother?"

She froze with her fork in the air. "You're kidding. I thought you got take-out?"

Antony shrugged. "I did in a way. I didn't make it, I got it from someone else."

Emory set her fork down. "No wonder you're so good at what you do. She's obviously amazing."

He smiled. "Tell her that and you'll be her friend for life. There's nothing my mother loves better than for people to love her cooking."

Emory laughed softly and continued eating. The candlelight danced across her cheeks and softened the sharp lines of her cheekbones, making her even more attractive than she already was.

Her coffee brown hair was pulled up in a messy bun on the top of her head, which Antony assumed she did whenever she was baking. But tendrils caressed the side and back of her neck, making him jealous of their freedom to do so.

"Oh my gosh…" Emory leaned back in her chair and rested a hand on her stomach. "I'm so full!"

"Not too full for dessert!" Antony asked, pretending to be aghast. "There's always room for sweets."

Emory smiled at him. "Usually I'm raring to go, but you might have to give me a push. I'm feeling rather lazy at the moment and way too full."

Antony grinned and stood up from his chair, reaching out a hand for her to take. When she slipped her hand into his, he gently lifted her from the table, giving her a little jerk at the last minute so that she stumbled into his chest. "Forgive me," he whispered as she pushed herself off of him.

"Sneak," she grumbled, straightening her shirt.

He chuckled. "Come on. Let's get started." He led her to a prepared tabletop where he'd left out the ingredients they would need.

"Sugar cookies?" she asked.

He nodded. "Yeah. Just a classic recipe with a couple of tweaks."

Emory rubbed her hands together. "Show me what to do, Chef."

"Want to cream the butter and sugar?" He pointed to a mixer.

"Aye, aye," she said, giving him a quick salute.

Antony kept an eye on her as he mixed the dry ingredients, enjoying watching her work. She moved easily, as if she had been in his kitchen her whole life, and he found himself feeling strangely content at sharing the space. His kitchen was his sanctuary and he was pretty picky about who he let work in it. In fact, other than his mother, Emory was the first person Antony had ever invited into his space. And as his chest warmed with desire and attraction, he found himself far from regretting it. "Ready?" he asked, forcing his thoughts to slow down.

She glanced over her shoulder. "Yep. It's nice and fluffy."

Antony brought the bowl of dry ingredients over and began to slowly dump in the flour and other supplies. Little by little, the separate ingredients began to turn into a nice dough. He turned off the mixer and brought it over to the counter. "Why don't you spread out some powdered sugar?"

"Ooh, we're going to roll it?" she asked as she followed his instructions.

"Yep."

"Do you have fun cookie cutters?" she asked with a grin. "I wish I'd known, because I actually collect them."

Antony raised his eyebrows as he dumped the dough onto the counter. "Really? What do you have?"

"Oh my gosh," she gushed. "I have almost everything. Antique ones, new ones. They're so cheap, and mostly small, that I have way more than any person would ever need."

He chuckled. "How many do you have?"

She scrunched up her nose. "I shouldn't admit that."

"Ah, come on. We're friends here," he pressed.

The mood became a little more serious as she looked at him. "You want to be friends?"

Antony held her gaze. "The best of everything begins with friendship."

Her small smile was the perfect response, then she answered his question. "Four hundred and seventy-three."

It took Antony a minute to digest the number she'd given him and when he did, he found himself laughing out loud. "You might have a problem."

She shrugged. "I know. But it's fun anyway."

He nodded, completely agreeing. Her addiction only made her more attractive. This evening was turning out to be everything he was hoping for.

CHAPTER 7

I can't believe I told him about my cookie cutter obsession. Way to make a guy think you're crazy. Emory shook her head, embarrassed, but knowing it was too late to do anything about it. The secret was out. "So...now what?" She gave him the floor. It was his kitchen after all.

"Now we roll it out and then we'll use those cookie cutters you're so fond of." He smiled as he patted the cookie dough into a large mound and Emory nearly sighed at the sight. He was soooo attractive and the swipe of flour on his cheek gave him a boyish innocence that sent Emory's heart to fluttering.

"Sounds good," she forced out, resting her hip against the counter and watching him work.

"What are you doing?" he asked with a frown.

Emory frowned back. "Watching."

He shook his head. "No way. We're in this together."

She pointed to his rolling pin. "That's a one-man job, unless you want to split the dough into two parts."

That delicious smirk crossed his face again. "Come here." He stepped back and indicated she should stand in front of him.

Her eyes widened when she realized what he had planned. She hesitated slightly, knowing that if she stepped into him, she would be giving a very clear signal of what she wanted in this relationship. *Am I ready for this? Do I want to say yes?* It had been a long time since she's started something with a man, and it was equal parts frightening and exciting. Taking a deep breath, she cautiously stepped in front of him, her pulse jumping when he closed her in.

"Ready?" he whispered in her ear.

"Not really," she admitted softly.

"I've made my interest known, Em," he continued. "The cookie is in your kitchen."

She laughed softly at his kitchen-ism. "It's been a long time," she told him.

"Is that a yes or no?"

She forced a long, slow breath into her lungs and back out again, pulling on her yoga practice to get her body to obey. She turned her head, his face only inches away. "I'm not the type of person who dates everything in my path."

"I never figured you were," he responded, his eyes studying hers.

"I'm afraid this won't mean as much to you as it would to me." There. She'd said it. Antony was attractive, a baker, and funny. But he also was smooth, sometimes too smooth, and it made Emory think that he flitted from one woman to the next without a care for their feelings.

His face grew serious. "I'm not a player, Emory. I won't say I haven't been on many dates, because I have, but it was only because I haven't found someone I wanted to stick around with."

"And what are your thoughts about us?"

He shrugged, his chest moving against her back. "I've found a woman who is beautiful, intriguing, and is constantly challenging me. Now I want to know her better. Is there anything wrong with that?"

She pinched her lips together. "No, there's not." She turned back to the dough, thoughts swirling through her brain. "So this is just for fun?"

"I don't know," he admitted. "There's no way you can't feel the chemistry between us," he said, leaning his cheek against the side of her head.

And it was true. She could feel it. The room temperature skyrocketed every time he came into sight. Her body responded to the sound of his voice and she often found herself wanting more. But those strong reactions would mean a much bigger fall if he decided he wanted to move on, and she was worried about setting herself up for heartache.

"I want to explore what we have. I've never been so intrigued before, so I don't know where this is going to lead. But I'm willing to find out. The question is...are you?"

It took Emory several seconds to answer. Pros and cons were running through her head like a hurricane, but one theme continued to stick out. She liked him. Genuinely liked him. Even though his arrogant teasing sometimes drove her a little crazy, she enjoyed their time together. And when he wasn't near her, she wanted him to be. *I guess that should be the only sign I need,* she admitted to herself. Straightening up, she grinned over her shoulder. "Are we baking cookies or what?"

Antony's smile was slow and made Emory warm all over. "Let me show you how I do it," he said, caging her in with his arms. He grabbed the wooden rolling pin and encouraged her to put her hands on it as well.

Emory was completely surrounded by him and was struggling to keep her mind on the task at hand. Slowly, they pressed into the dough, lengthening it out until it was thin enough to cut.

"I may not have the collection of cutters you do," Antony said, reaching away from her and across the counter, "but since Christmas is coming, I figured that's what we should stick with."

"When did you make that elf?" Emory found herself asking. Thinking of the holiday had brought back memories of the poster she had seen when she'd first walked in.

"That was last year for a hotel reception," he answered.

"It's magnificent."

"Thank you." Antony handed her the snowman shape. "You cut those ones, I'll do the trees." He rested one hand on her waist as he leaned forward to press the cutter into the dough. "Did you know you smell like cinnamon and nutmeg?"

Emory laughed, slightly embarrassed. "I think it's a hazard of the job."

He ran his nose along her ear, sending massive goosebumps down her neck. "You mean it's a perk of the job." He kissed the spot right under her lobe. "How has your headache been?"

"My what?" Emory whispered hoarsely. Right now her mind couldn't think of anything but him. The touch of his lips against her skin and the sensations that were rioting throughout her body.

"Your headache. You're always rubbing your temples whenever you get stressed," he whispered, his lips still touching her skin.

"I...don't know," she stammered. *Oh my gosh, this is so embarrassing, but who can think straight during this kind of assault?*

He chuckled, the vibrations coming through her back. Letting go of the cookie cutter, he put his other hand on her waist and slowly turned her around. "That was a perfect answer," he said, leaning down until their mouths were just shy of touching. "Let me help you keep it away."

"Please do," Emory said in a barely audible voice right before their mouths met. *Oh...my...goodness...* were the last logical thoughts that ran through Emory's head before sensation took over.

NO WONDER I CAN'T GET her out of my head. Antony might have been fairly active on the dating scene, but never once had his body reacted when he kissed a girl as it was right now. Emory's thin frame was pressed up against his chest and his arms were all the way around her, keeping her tucked as close as he could get her. Her hands were clenching his shirt at the shoulders, while their mouths met together in a dance that seemed as if they had been doing it their whole lives.

He'd never had any woman feel so...perfect. His arms tightened around her and his kisses grew more intense until he heard her gasp slightly. Forcing his limbs into submission, Antony slowed down and eased his hold.

"Sorry," he panted, straightening up, his chest still heaving with emotion. "I got carried away."

Her light blue eyes were wide, but she nodded. "It's okay."

Antony chuckled. She was simply too cute for her own good. "I suppose we should get back to making cookies, huh? I did promise you dessert."

"I think I already had it," Emory muttered.

Antony's eyebrows shot up before he burst out laughing. "If you're worried about me being arrogant before, you need to watch what you say. Comments like that will only make it worse."

Emory rolled her eyes and turned back to the cookie dough. "This stuff is going to dry out if we don't get moving."

Still chuckling, Antony leaned into her back again and reached around to press the cutter into the dough over and over again. Once they had a full sheet, he picked it up and walked it over to one of the ovens.

"I'm guessing eight or ten minutes on three-fifty," Emory called out behind him.

Antony put the cookies in, then sauntered back toward her, leaning down for a quick kiss on her nose. "That's because you're one smart cookie."

She groaned. "I can't believe you just said that."

Antony laughed. "Someone had to use it. It's been sitting there all evening just waiting to be picked up."

"I would've thought someone with your level of artistic talent would be a little more refined in their humor," she said primly, going back to the cookie dough.

Antony took his favorite place right behind her and whispered in her ear, "Never underestimate the power of a good pun. Even the haters usually end up smiling."

She peered over her shoulder. "That's because we can't believe how bad they are sometimes."

He shrugged. "I make no apologies. I've heard some good ones over the years and I will always collect them."

"It's a wonder we're friends," she grumbled good-naturedly.

"So you decided that's what we are?" He watched her chew on her bottom lip, sucking it in and out a couple of times as she contemplated.

"Yes," she finally responded, but she wouldn't meet his gaze. "Though I don't usually go around kissing my friends."

"Ah...but the best kissers are ones who started out as friends," he argued.

"Then what does that make us?" she teased. "We didn't originally start out as friends."

He nodded. "True. I've never had a friend accuse me of theft before."

She paused in her work. "Again...I'm sorry about that. I was frustrated and angry, and you seemed the most likely target."

He brought the edge of his jaw to rest against the side of her head. "I get it. I didn't like it, but I get it. I'm sorry it got eaten."

She sighed and nodded. "Yeah, me too. The woman Hank took in used to work at the inn." Emory squished her lips to the side. "In fact, I met her when I first got to town and needed to buy some candy. I went to the Sugar Shoppe. What I don't get is why she was stealing jewelry, but I'm hoping that her arrest will be an end to all the weird things going on in the inn right now."

"What else has been happening?" Antony asked, intrigued.

"Don't you remember? All the missing food, the stolen items, and we keep finding stuff out of place."

"Oh, yeah," he agreed, nodding. "I'd forgotten about the other stuff." His brows furrowed together as he thought of the situation. "It seems weird that that girl would do all those things. Do you think she was starving? I mean, she lost her job, right? But if she was hungry, why steal sweets? As an adult woman, I'd expect her to take regular meals rather than the desserts."

Emory shrugged. "I don't know, but does it matter? She was stealing. That's all there was to it." A buzzing sound caught her attention and Emory looked over at her purse.

"Need to get that?" Antony asked, disappointed they were being interrupted.

Emory thought for a moment. "I should at least check it. Hope got back from the hospital this evening. It might have to do with her."

Antony nodded and backed up so she could go get her phone.

She studied the screen, scrolling down slowly. "It looks like Detective Hank will be at the house in the morning. He'll tell us everything that he's uncovered."

Antony made a face. "I'll be baking."

She nodded, typing out a quick reply, then stuffing the phone back in her purse. "I can get you all the info." She paused and looked at him. "If you want?"

He nodded. "That would be great, thanks." He walked over to her and looked at her mouth. "I'm sure my mother will eventually let me know everything, but I'd much rather hear it from" —he gave her a slow, lingering kiss— "this mouth."

"You are way too good at that," she said breathlessly.

"What? Kissing a beautiful woman?"

She shook her head. "No. Making me feel like you actually care."

Antony frowned. "What do you mean? You don't think this is real?" He stepped back, feeling like she'd slapped him in the face. "I told you before, I'm not a player. I don't just toy with women like they're made for my personal amusement."

Emory deflated and rubbed her temples again. "I'm sorry, Antony. I don't really mean it like that, it's just...this is fast. Or at least it feels fast. I know we've known each other a few weeks now, but up until a few days ago, we argued every time we were in the same room."

He put his hands in the air. "That's not exactly my fault."

She gave him a look. "You and your ego didn't exactly try to stop it either."

They both turned to the oven when the timer went off. Waiting to answer her, Antony took the time to get the cookies out, as a chance to cool down his frustration. It felt like he'd taken one step forward then two steps backs. He slapped the hot metal against the counter top. "All you have to do is say the word, Em," he finally responded. "Say the word and I'll back off." He picked up his head and gave her a hard stare. "Excuse me if I'm wrong, but I could have sworn just a bit ago, you admitted to being interested in seeing where this could go between us."

"I know," she said, regret lacing her tone. "I'm sorry. I'm just scared. You tie me up in knots and I can't think straight." She pushed her hands into her hair, nearly dislodging the bun on top of her hair. "I've spent my whole life being logical. I've pushed men and distractions to the backburner so that I could focus on making a name for myself. After culinary school, it was all about opening my own storefront. Then I thought I was catching a break by coming to take over for Grandma." She waved a hand in his direction. "And now you show up, with your gorgeous hair and smoldering eyes, and you turn my stomach into knots. I can barely focus because I'm always listening for my phone to see if you're going to text. I find myself smiling when I think about something you've said or done." She blew out a raspberry with her lips. "I feel equal parts stupid and special." She threw both hands in the air. "Can you blame me for having second thoughts?"

Antony couldn't stop his smirk as he walked back to her. "Let's just take it one step at a time, huh?" he asked softly as he gave her a light kiss. "And it's very important that we get back to those cookies."

She frowned. "Why is that?"

"Because I have every intention of eating the frosting off your lips and proving to you that this is worth pursuing." He chuckled at the shocked look on her face. "Ready?"

"Nope," she whispered. "But I'll give it a try."

CHAPTER 8

E mory found herself humming as she worked the next day. Her kitchen had been extremely busy that morning with the meeting with the detective, and though he had given everyone good news, he'd also dropped a bomb that had upset the entire family.

Trisha wasn't the only thief.

And there were secret passages in the inn.

Trisha had admitted to taking Mrs. Harrison's ring and messing with Hope's cart and supplies. However, the issues with food, tools, and gardening gear were not done by her. Enoch had found a secret attic with Emory's pie plate inside and a few other items that suggested someone was living behind the walls of Gingerbread Inn.

Despite the news, Emory found herself in a very good mood, which seemed odd given the circumstances. She had just found out there was another criminal running around, eating her food and stealing her baked goods, but she couldn't seem to wipe the smile off her face.

"You're so gone," she grumbled to herself as she finished one last detail on her window. "There." She stood and stretched out her neck, rubbing it with her free hand. She'd been bent over all morning, working on the tiny details left for her gingerbread house. Now she was feeling it in her back and shoulders.

"Let me help you," a smooth, deep voice said behind her.

Emory squeaked when a large, warm hand joined her at the back of her neck and began to massage her skin. Emory closed her eyes and let her head hang. "You do realize half of that tension is from you scaring me?" she grumbled, making Antony laugh.

He leaned close enough that she could smell the yeasty fragrance of fresh bread. "Can you blame me for wanting an excuse to touch you?"

Emory laughed breathlessly, then shook off his hand and turned around. They looked at each other for a moment and she realized his smile was just as goofy as hers was. "Hey," she said softly.

"Hay is for horses," he retorted with a chuckle. "I was thinking of something more like this." Without hesitation, he leaned in for a sweet kiss.

Emory knew that the idea of butterflies erupting in her stomach was completely cliche, but there was nothing else to compare it to. Flutters ran through her entire midsection and she found her breathing growing shallow and quick. "That works too," she whispered when he pulled back.

Antony laughed and took her hand. "Show me what you're working on."

She frowned. "You sure you want to see? I mean, I know you already saw some stuff you shouldn't have, but it really is supposed to be a surprise."

He shrugged. "You don't have to show me, but I love watching you work. And your house was amazing before. I can only imagine what you've done to it since then."

A warm flush worked its way up her neck and Emory ducked her head. "One of these days, I'll make you show me your creation as payback."

"Done." He kissed the top of her head. "You can see it tonight when you come over to finish our cookies."

Emory couldn't help but laugh, a wonderful lightness bubbling through her. "What? Didn't you get your fill of frosting last night?" Her mind's eye flashed picture after picture of him kissing her during their semi-date last night. It had been a heady, wondrous experience. A time when Emory had let down her guard and gone with the flow, which was completely foreign to her. And she had loved it. Her burdens felt lighter and her soul felt freer than it ever had before. It had left her with a craving for more. In that exact moment, she thought she just might get it.

His eyes could only be described as smoldering when he looked at her. "I don't know if I'll ever get my fill," he said seriously.

Emory's gulped. *Holy cow, I think he's serious!*

He squeezed her hand. "So come on. Show me."

"Okay, but remember," she wagged a finger at him, "you asked for it."

He smiled. "I'll take my chances."

Emory turned and opened up the view to the table she'd been working at. She watched Antony study her work. "I was trying to add a snowy affect," she said softly, shifting her weight from side to side. She wasn't exactly sure why, but Antony's opinion of her work was important to her. She knew she had a crush on him, but they'd only truly been together for a day, which made it bizarre that his opinion mattered, but there it was.

He shook his head slowly and her heart fell. "That's amazing," he breathed. He pointed to her work on the corner of the roof. "It looks so realistic in that dripping technique. How can you have such a steady hand?" When he turned to look at her, his eyes were shining with something suspiciously like admiration, and Emory felt herself warm all over again.

She shrugged. "I don't know. I just do it. How do you take a hunk of chocolate and turn it into an elf that looks alive?"

He shrugged. "It's a gift."

Emory shook her head with a smile, then slugged his shoulder. "There's that ego I was missing."

He caught her hand and used it to tug her toward him. "Don't worry. I'll make sure to keep it where you can see it."

Emory rolled her eyes, but was secretly amused. While he talked a big game, she was coming more and more to know that he just enjoyed stirring the pot a little. He liked to tease and see people's reactions, especially hers.

"So...what can I help with?" Antony asked, looking around the room. "I have to say I'm surprised the presentation room isn't done."

Emory sighed and followed his gaze. Wooden platforms were in varying stages of construction, and the lights around the room had been hung, but others that would go on the table were still rolled into circles. The tree in the corner was waiting to be decorated and the model train set was still boxed up. "I know," she said in a depressed tone. "With all the craziness going on at the inn, I haven't done as much as I should, and Enoch has been busy trying to catch the culprit. Now he's helping Hope get back on her feet."

"Speaking of which," Antony pressed, "are we all in the clear?"

"I wish." Emory shook her head. "Trisha only stole the ring and messed with Hope. She claims she didn't have anything to do with the food or the tools."

Antony frowned and scratched his chin. "So we have two thieves?"

She shrugged. "I guess. But who's to say? Maybe she just doesn't want to admit she took those things?"

Antony shook his head. "No. That doesn't make sense. Stealing a pie or some nougat is much less criminal than jewelry. Not to mention she nearly killed your cousin."

Emory deflated and her chin sunk to her chest. She didn't stay that way for long though, as Antony took it upon him to pull her into his strong arms and rub her back. It felt so soothing that Emory immediately melted into his chest and relaxed. "I don't know what to do," she admitted in a small voice.

"Don't worry about it now," he urged. "Let me help you here and we'll just try to take it one step at a time, hmm?"

Taking a deep breath, Emory finally nodded. "Thank you."

He pushed her back gently and gazed into her eyes. "Anytime."

ANTONY KNEW HE WAS getting too serious, too fast with this girl, but there was little to be done about it now. Their kiss yesterday had shifted something in him. He almost burned a batch of croissants this morning because all he could think of was Emory and the way she felt in his arms.

He hadn't burnt his pastries in years and now suddenly he could barely remember how to make the dough. Antony chuckled to himself. *I'm like a young boy with his first crush. Mom better not find out about this or I'll get a tongue-lashing.*

"How are you with power tools?" Emory asked.

Antony grinned. "I use them all the time with my sculptures, so I can hold my own."

Emory smiled at him and his pulse kicked into gear. "Great. Do you think we can get the rest of the tables built?"

He nodded. "Of course." He looked at his hands. "You don't happen to have some gloves, do you?"

She shook her head. "No, but Enoch probably does."

"The handyman?" Antony asked.

She nodded.

"Never mind. I've got a few inches on him, so I'll bet my hands are bigger."

She scrunched up her nose. "I'm sorry. All I've got are oven mitts."

"It's no big deal," he assured her. "I'm just being a baby."

"I don't want you getting splinters though."

Antony reached out and put his knuckles under her chin. He shouldn't have brought up the gloves to begin with. Emory tended to worry about things, and he could see the line between her eyebrows growing deeper. "I'll be fine. I shouldn't have even asked." Cupping the side of her face, he pushed at the wrinkle she was creating. "Relax and let's just get to work, okay?"

She gave him a sheepish grin. "Okay."

"Great." He reluctantly dropped his touch. "Where should we start?"

Emory shrugged. "Umm...I'm not much of a builder, so I was hoping you could lead the way."

"Sounds good to me." Antony surveyed the room once more. "Let's start here, and work our way around to the end of the displays, huh?"

"You're the boss," she quipped.

"I like the sound of that," Antony shot back, smiling when she laughed. "Okay. Put on your big girl muscles and help me lift this board onto the frame." They worked together for several minutes in silence, and only the sound of drills humming and the squealing of screws going through plywood could be heard. "Since we're going to be here for a while, you might as well tell me your story," Antony grunted as he lay on his back, pressing a screw into a table leg.

"My story?" she asked.

"Yeah. You know that I didn't go to culinary school. That I was an art geek and that my mother can cook like a professional. Now tell me about you. Siblings? Why baking? Why are you slaving away in a hotel and not sharing your talents with the world?"

"I'm not sure I should answer that," Emory grumbled. "Some of it was decidedly offensive."

Antony gave her a wide grin, then crawled to his knees in order to put the screw through the top of the table. "Or maybe it was a recognition of your abilities and a push of support for you to do what your heart desires."

She made a face at him. "How do you know what my heart desires?"

Antony let his right eyebrow raise very slowly, along with the smile on his face. "Do you really want me to answer that?"

Emory turned away from him and cleared her throat. "Nope. Nope and nope. Forget I asked."

He laughed quietly as she regained her composure. "You did mention that you wanted to open a storefront," he said casually. "I gathered the unappreciated part from the fact that you don't like to talk about work."

Emory made a face at his observations. "I have to admit to being a product of my grandmother's time and energy." She let out a happy, contented sigh. "Whenever we came to visit at the inn, she always took me into the kitchen and we baked together. Bread...cookies...cakes...you name it, we did it."

"Always sweet stuff?"

Emory shook her head. "No. We did dinner and other stuff as well, but the treats were my favorite." She gave a breathy laugh. "I had to learn to put exercise into my routine really quickly when I went to college or else I'd have ended up as big as a house."

Antony tsked his tongue. "A beautiful woman is beautiful no matter what her size," he scolded.

Emory blushed again and turned away from him. "Thank you," she said softly.

"You're welcome. Now, let's grab the next one."

Emory followed orders and they began working on the next part of the table.

"Continue," he said as they settled into routine.

"There's really not much to tell. I think Grandma recognized that I'm sort of...technique-driven—"

"A perfectionist?" he offered.

She gave him a sarcastic smile. "Yes. A perfectionist. Happy?"

Antony nodded. "I am now. That was perfect."

It took her a second, but Emory snorted a laugh. "You're ridiculous."

"I try, but I really do want to hear the rest."

She took a deep breath. "With Grandma's encouragement, I headed straight to culinary school after high school and worked my way through it. Of course, I was especially interested in the baking parts."

"Of course."

She grinned at him. "After I graduated, I began at the bottom. I'm working my way up. I work in a big hotel in Seattle. We do catering and have a restaurant inside the hotel."

"And do you get credit for your creations?"

The happiness she'd displayed a moment before disappeared. "No. But I've gained lots of experience."

"Experience is good," Antony said, pausing his work and folding his arms across the table. "But sometimes you have to take a leap of faith."

Her eyes grew misty and she quickly turned away, blinking and sniffling.

Antony immediately felt bad. He hadn't meant to make her cry, but he knew all too well what it was like to work under someone who never let you shine or use your creative abilities. He'd nearly suffocated in a job doing that. It was what had pushed him to open a storefront so quickly in his career. He refused to let another "expert" have control over his talent, and he wanted the same for Emory. Her food was amazing, and the way she nurtured those around her with it was a sign that it wasn't just a job, it was her heart and soul. She could do so much better than hiding in another's shadow. "I'm sorry," he said softly. "I wasn't try—"

"What's going on in here?" a woman's voice snapped shrilly. "The Gingerbread competition is in ten days and you haven't even finished the room?"

Emory gasped and Antony had to school his face to keep from scowling at the intrusive, rude woman who was standing in the doorway.

"H-hello Mrs. Pearson," Emory said, putting herself together quickly. "Things have been a little intense around here, but Antony and I are working on it now."

The older woman peered down her nose at Antony and he smiled back, though he had no desire to. "Why are you always here instead of in town at your shop?" She sneered. "Perhaps you're lacking in business?"

Antony bit back a smart remark. If his mother hadn't been such a dragon about manners when he was growing up, he'd have let this woman have it.

She sniffed. "I don't know why you came to Seagull Cove, anyway. Don't need someone like you when the rest of us can bake perfectly well ourselves."

Sometimes I hate small towns, he thought bitterly. "Don't worry, Mrs. Pearson. I have no intention of sharing my baked goods with you at all, so it shouldn't be a problem." He smiled again when Mrs. Pearson bristled and Emory's eyes about bugged out of her head. *Take that and stuff it,* he thought, but used his last bit of self-control to keep from saying it out loud.

CHAPTER 9

Emory nearly choked on her own tongue. *What is he doing? You NEVER poke the bear! Especially one as cantankerous as Mrs. Pearson.* Deciding it was best to divert the older woman's attention before she gathered more ammunition to shoot at Antony, Emory stepped forward. "What can I help you with today?" she asked as politely as she could manage.

Mrs. Pearson's mouth flapped open and closed a few more times and her face was a dangerous shade of puce, but she managed to turn to Emory and clamp her jaw shut. "This is exactly why we don't like outsiders in our town," she hissed. "No respect. No respect at all."

Ignoring Antony's snort, Emory spoke a little louder to try and hide his amusement. "Can I get you something to drink? Some tea, perhaps? Or a cookie? I baked some fresh this morning."

"As if I'd eat anything of yours," Mrs. Pearson said primly. "You probably cook like your grandmother."

Ooh, Emory was struggling now. She could handle mean girls, or in this case a mean woman, but she didn't handle people insulting her grandmother. Claire Simmons was a saint. She had kept a family business going for decades, even with being a wife and mother. She'd raised wonderful children and was now involved in her grandchildren's lives. It was because Grandma Claire was so wonderful that her three granddaughters had come running to help during her time of need. "Mrs. Pearson," Emory said tightly. "I'll ask again why you came. If it was simply to insult my family or complain about new businesses, then you can take those words elsewhere, because I have no desire to hear them."

"Well…" Mrs. Pearson huffed. "You're your grandmother's posterity through and through." She shook her head. "No manners at all in you young people."

Emory forced down the words she wanted to say and conjured a fake smile instead. "Since you don't seem to have any real business here, I'd be happy to walk you to the door."

"You will not," Mrs. Pearson snapped, tugging on her shirt sleeves. "I've come to make sure you took my advice about the set-up so that my house will be seen to its best advantage." She squinted up. "The lights are far too dark in here. I'll need a spotlight."

"Mrs. Pearson," Emory explained, "no one will be getting an individual spotlight. The lights will be dim because we are using Christmas lights, just like they have done every year. There will be more lights around the gingerbread displays, but no one will be given special treatment." Emory relaxed slightly when she felt a strong presence at her back. Surely with Antony standing behind her, Mrs. Pearson would back off.

"Your grandmother gave herself special treatment every year," Mrs. Pearson accused. "Always coming in first, while my displays were always second." Her lip curled a little. "And now your boyfriend here is trying to get his own special treatment by cozying up to you while you work."

Emory could feel the anger coming off of Antony, and although she, herself, was also struggling with her own emotions, she was afraid some real damage would be done if she didn't stop this now. "Mrs. Pearson," she said firmly, "it's time for you to go home."

"Not until I have a look around."

Emory could feel her nostrils flaring, but she held her tongue. There was nothing to be gained by fighting back, and the contestants did have a right to see the display area. "That's fine," Emory said, her jaw slightly clenched. "However, any more unkind remarks and I'll be calling Sheriff Davidson."

Mrs. Pearson grumbled something about the sheriff being in Claire's pocket before she finally began to walk around the space.

Emory stood with her arms crossed and watched every move the woman made.

"You're nicer than me," Antony whispered in her ear.

Emory ignored the goosebumps his nearness brought and focused on the situation at hand. "No. I've just learned how to deal with haters more than you."

He scrunched his eyebrows. "You think I haven't dealt with that?"

Emory glanced up at him. "Probably. But being a woman in a man's world means I've handled my fair share of bullies."

He shrugged, then grinned. "I'll give you that, but it doesn't negate the fact that you were kinder than you had to be."

"Best thing to do with bullies is to be firm in your own beliefs," she said back. "Anger answered with anger doesn't fix it."

"Maybe not, but it can sure help you feel better," he grumbled.

Emory huffed a quiet laugh, but it fell quickly from her face when she heard a crash. She gasped and looked over to see Mrs. Pearson looking distraught...sort of.

"Oh, dear me," she twittered. "I seemed to have bumped into something here."

Emory felt herself sway when she realized it was one of the panels to her house. She'd forgotten some her work was out here, and Mrs. Pearson had just bumped her work table, knocking a piece of it to the floor.

"What kind of game are you playing?" Antony growled, storming over to the unwelcome woman.

She appeared to quiver under his anger and Emory couldn't blame her. Antony looked ready to tear her apart. "It was an accident!" Mrs. Pearson defended, slinking back. "You shouldn't have left your work out in the open if you wanted it safe." She straightened her shoulders, though it was easy to see she was shaking slightly. "I haven't been steady on my feet in years. It couldn't be helped."

"Get out," Antony said through clenched teeth.

"What?" Mrs. Pearson said breathlessly.

Emory stood frozen in her anxiety and shock as Antony towered over the woman. "Get. Out," he said in a low, dangerous voice. "You'll be lucky if you aren't kicked out of the competition for this. I doubt the committee will take kindly to sabotaging your competitors."

Mrs. Pearson gasped in outrage. "Accidents have nothing to do with sabotage." She seemed to regain her courage and her eyes narrowed first at Antony, then Emory. "You won't be able to prove anything. Take this to the committee and I'll be sure to inform the newspaper about all the troubles you've been having here at the inn." She grinned in smug satisfaction. "I'm sure you wouldn't want the *reputation* of your precious bed and breakfast to become all about criminals and stolen jewelry, would you?"

Emory balked at the threat. "How do you know about that?" she demanded.

Antony also chimed in. "I'd be happy to drive you to the police station so you can share the information you have," he said with a sneer. "I'm sure the sheriff would be eager to know where you got your information."

Mrs. Pearson's lip curled again. "I can see my way out, thank you." Sticking her nose in the air, she walked out of the room without a single wobble in her supposedly unsteady gait.

As soon as the woman was out of sight, Emory's vision filled with tears. "My house," she whispered thickly. "My house." She heard Antony run toward her just as her knees gave out, catching her in his arms.

ANTONY REPOSITIONED his arms to get a better hold on Emory, and tucked her under his chin. "It's gonna be okay," he whispered into her hair. "It's gonna be okay."

"How?" Emory asked, her voice broken and far from the usual strength of will she possessed. "I worked on that for weeks, Antony! Weeks! I know I shouldn't have left it out, but I was feeling claustrophobic in the kitchen and needed a little air." She straightened and sniffled. "There's no way I can remake that part of my house in such a short time. What will people think?" Her watery eyes looked up to him as if he held all the answers, but Antony had nothing. "Grandma has won for years, and now the one time she passes the whisk to her granddaughter, she fails." Her bottom lip began to tremble harder and Antony palmed the back of her head and held her close again.

"Have a good cry," he said softly, his heart breaking for her loss. *This should never have happened.* Even while he felt terrible for Emory, he was ready to strangle Mrs. Pearson. That woman had had it in for him ever since he arrived in Seagull Cove. The residents who lived there year-round had been slightly standoffish when he'd arrived, but were slowly warming up to him. Tourists, of course, had no problem stopping in his shop. But Mrs. Pearson had been a different story. Not only had she made her complaints about his bakery, she had worked hard to convince others he was a terrible baker as well.

Luckily, most of the residents didn't listen to her, but it still bugged Antony. *What right does she have to treat people like that? To ruin others' lives?* Antony looked over at the shattered gingerbread and he nearly saw red. His protective instincts were screaming at him, but it was too late. The damage had already been done.

"What am I going to do?" she asked, leaning back from him once more. Emory turned and faced the broken house. Slowly, she stepped out of his embrace and walked over to kneel on the floor.

Antony let her go reluctantly. His mind screamed that he wasn't done comforting or taking care of her, but really...what more could he do? There seemed to be only one direction. "Rebuild."

She looked at him sadly. "There isn't time."

Antony walked over and squatted down beside her. "So make time."

She laughed harshly and wiped at her eyes. "I can't just make more hours in the day, Antony."

"No, but you can use more of them. And you're not alone. I'll continue working in here while you go bake another wall."

She gave him a sad smile and brushed her fingers along his jawline, sending little shocks of electricity through his skin. "It's a good thought, but I just don't see how it's possible."

Grabbing her hand, Antony raised them both to their feet. "So we'll make it possible." He could see she still wasn't convinced and he felt a surge of desperation that she not give up. He wasn't sure why it was so important to him that she fulfill this challenge, but it was. "Come on, Em. Take a chance. A leap of faith." He smiled encouragingly. "What does it hurt to try?"

She didn't return his smile. "But what if I fail? The odds are stacked against me."

"You already told me you were a woman in a man's world," he said, brushing a piece of hair off her forehead. "Since you're here, you've already won. Nothing can stop you."

She sighed and glanced at the ground. "It'll be almost impossible to match what I've done already."

"I have faith in you," he said.

She gave a watery chuckle. "I suppose that means I should have faith in myself?"

Antony shrugged. "It doesn't hurt."

Emory nodded and took in a shuddering breath. "I suppose you're right. I don't really have anything to lose at this point."

He gave her a smirk and kissed her temple. "I think I could listen to those words all day."

"Jerk," she said in a teasing tone, smacking his chest with the back of her hand.

"If by jerk, you mean I'm a wonderful boyfriend...then yes, you're correct."

She eyed him. "That's a big jump."

He wrapped his arms around her again. "It's the only way for us, Em. We don't do anything in small increments."

She laughed lightly. "I suppose not."

"Now...we need to talk about who to report Mrs. Pearson to. I know you're on the committee, so you probably know the right person to talk to."

Emory shook her head. "I'm not reporting her."

"What?" Antony jerked back. "You can't let her get away with this!"

Emory raised her eyebrows at his shouting. "I can," she stated firmly. "Nothing will be gained by building a dispute. My grandmother still lives in this town, and so do you. If Mrs. Pearson is ostracized because of this, it will only make life harder on everyone."

He shook his head. "I understand your logic, but I can't agree with it."

"That's all right." Emory patted his shoulder. "You don't have to. Being together doesn't mean you get to make my choices for me."

"Au contraire," he said with a grin that widened when Emory shot him a sharp look. "I'm about to make a decision for the two of us right now."

"Oh, really?"

Antony pressed his lips to hers before she could say any more with him and couldn't help but smile during their kiss when she joined in without argument.

"This doesn't make you right," she whispered against his lips.

"It certainly didn't make me wrong," he whispered before kissing her again. He let himself get lost in her only for a few moments before separating. "Come on. Let's get you baking, and I'll get building."

Emory took another deep breath. "Okay. Let's do this."

They walked hand in hand into the kitchen, jerking to a stop when Emory gasped. "What?" Antony asked with a frown. He looked around but didn't see anything amiss.

"It can't be her. Can it?" Emory asked, dropping his hand and rushing to the far counter.

"Em...what's going on?" he asked, coming up behind her.

"Look." Emory pointed to the counter and suddenly Antony understood. Loaves of apple cinnamon bread were stacked neatly next to each other, cooling from the oven. Right in the middle of the row was an empty spot on the cooling rack, though small bits of the sweet bread had been left behind on the rack.

"You think Mrs. Pearson is the one who's been stealing all the food?" Antony asked. He scrunched up his nose. "That doesn't make any sense. Why would she do that?"

"I don't know," Emory argued. "But you saw her ruin my house, and now my bread is missing." She folded her arms over her chest. "Don't you find it a little suspicious?"

Antony nodded thoughtfully. "Yeah, I do. But I still can't see a good reason. Breaking your house is one thing. She wants to win the competition. But stealing your food?" He shook his head. "I don't see it. Not to mention, how would she have gotten around without being seen?"

Emory pinched her lips into a small, white line. "I don't know, but I want to find out."

CHAPTER 10

"What are you going to do?" Antony asked, leaning his hip against the counter. "Confront her?"

Emory began to pace. Everything was so crazy right now. She needed to remake her house, or at least she needed to remake one of the walls. She needed to catch a thief, and she needed to keep everyone else from finding out. Finally she shook her head. "No. I can't risk it right now."

"What do you mean?" he asked, frowning.

"I don't want anyone to know what's going on," Emory stated, stopping her movements. "I don't want my cousins or Grandma to worry about any of this, and if I go after Mrs. Pearson, it'll bring everything into the light."

Antony's frown deepened. "I understand not accusing her until you have more evidence, but I don't understand keeping it quiet. What's the purpose? Mrs. Pearson already knew stuff was going on, so how do you know the rest of the town doesn't know as well?"

Emory sighed and rubbed at her temples. "Since Mrs. Pearson was threatening to tell everyone, I'm guessing it's not common knowledge yet. Grandma is recovering from surgery, Antony. She's worried about her inn and trying to train all of us girls on what to do. Not to mention, it's nearly Christmas, her inn is full, and the stress level is high. I'm not going to add to that if I can help it."

Antony slowly shook his head. "I don't like it. I think it would be better to let your family help you."

Emory shook her head back, more emphatically. "I can't. Hope is still recovering from her ordeal and Bella would shout it all to the world. That's the last thing I need."

He sighed and pinched the bridge of his nose. "So it's just me and you?"

Emory smiled and walked up to him, resting her hands against his chest. "I guess so," she said softly. She could see the hesitation in his gray eyes, but she really needed him to agree to keep quiet. Grandma Claire was older and already recovering from a difficult medical emergency. And none of what Emory had mentioned covered the fact that Grandma's sister's family was trying to sue for the inn. This was definitely not the time to tell Grandma that Emory thought they were being sabotaged by a woman in town. "Think you can handle us having a secret?" she whispered, walking her fingers up to his neck.

He grinned, and Emory knew her little seduction wasn't fooling anybody, but she was grateful nonetheless when he nodded with a resigned sigh. He wrapped his arms around her waist. "I might be able to be convinced to stay silent," he said with a quirked brow.

Emory smiled. "What will it cost me?"

He brought their noses together. "A kiss any time I want." He gave her a light kiss. "And as many as I want." He kissed her again.

"That's quite a high price," she said breathlessly, enjoying the jumping sensations in her stomach.

"You're asking for a high amount of self-control," he continued, his lips skimming along her jawline. "It requires a high amount of recompense."

"I suppose I can handle that," Emory agreed. She brought her hands up around his neck. "Are you wanting one right now?"

"Yes," he said, giving her a quick peck. "And no."

Emory jerked back a little with a frown. "What?"

He gave her a crooked grin. "Do I want one? Yes, more than one, in fact. But I want to see you succeed at your gingerbread house more." Grabbing her shoulders, he turned her around and gave her a swat on her backside. "Go bake. I'll go build."

Emory gave him a teasing scowl, then headed to the cupboards. Before opening them, she took a deep breath. "You can do this," she whispered to herself. "You've just got to work a little harder. It'll all work out."

"Darn right it will!" Antony called as he headed out the door and into the adjoining display room.

Emory smiled, unable to help herself. Normally she took on all her challenges herself, but there was something decidedly nice about having a support system. She found her smile stayed as she mixed all the ingredients together, scraping the last of the molasses out of her jar in order to create the cookie dough. She worked quickly, noting the sounds of the drill every few minutes. Every once in a while there would be a loud squeak as the screw was pressed into the plywood and Emory would cringe, grateful she wasn't inside the room with him.

"Hey, cuz," Bella greeted from the entrance. "Whatcha up to?"

Emory smiled over her shoulder, hoping Bella didn't look too closely at her project. "Just...baking some gingerbread."

"Oooh, can I try some?" Bella walked over and reached for the dough.

"Nope," Emory said, softly slapping Bella's hand away. "This is the construction kind. No eating."

Bella frowned. "Wait a second. Why are you making more of that? I thought your house was almost done."

"It...was," Emory said carefully, turning away and keeping her eyes on the dough. She carefully cut around her paper outline she'd used previously to get the right shape for the house.

"Em."

"Hmm?"

"Spill it."

Emory frowned and turned around. "What?"

Bella gave her a "really?" look. "Are you serious? You think you can keep something from me?" She grinned and slowly shook her head.

"I'm actually a little offended that you think I wouldn't notice something was wrong."

Emory scowled. "I don't have to tell you everything."

"You don't," Bella said carefully. "But you should." She winked. "We both know I'll figure it out anyway."

Emory snorted. "I don't think being nosy should be a good thing."

Bella studied her nails. "What can I say? It's the mark of a Pulitzer Prize-winning journalist."

"You haven't won that," Emory said drily.

"Yet," Bella added. "Since I have the qualifications, we both know it's only a matter of time."

"Hey, Em?" Antony walked back into the kitchen, his hands full of the broken house. "Do you want me to—?" He paused and his eyes widened. "Oh...hey, Bella."

Bella turned her head and purposefully looked at Emory before facing Antony again. "Hello, Antony. Been here long?"

"Uh..." He cleared his throat and shifted his weight from one side to the other. "Just helping out. Enoch's been a bit busy, I guess."

Bella nodded. "Yep. He's smooching our other cousin to help her 'recover.'" She used her fingers to create quotations.

"Bella..." Emory scolded. "Leave them alone."

Bella grinned. "Just like you want me to leave you and Antony alone?"

Emory scowled. "Maybe how you'd like me to leave you and Detective Hank alone." She grinned when Bella turned pink. "Not so fun when the tables are turned, is it?"

Bella put her hands in the air. "I get it. We're all holding our love cards close to the chest."

Emory groaned and hung her head while Antony chuckled.

"But trying to distract me from the fact that Antony is holding a broken gingerbread house won't work," Bella stated, growing serious. Her blue eyes bore into Emory's. "What happened?"

ANTONY'S EYES DARTED from Bella to Emory and back. He wasn't sure if he should speak up or just stay quiet and let Emory handle her cousin. They should have known better than to think they could keep everything quiet, though. Bella was always trying to scrape out a good story and Emory should've thought of that. *Or maybe I should've looked before walking back into the kitchen,* he thought wryly.

"One of the panels of my house broke," Emory said, slumping against the counter. "I'm trying to make a new one."

Bella whistled low. "Geez. That's gotta be stressful. You've been working on that thing since we got here." She bit her lip. "Do you have time to redo it?"

Emory shrugged. "I don't know, but I figure I've got to try." She glanced at Antony. He smiled and gave her a nod.

"Awesome." Bella rubbed her hands together. "What can I do to help?"

Emory sighed and Antony knew she was grateful Bella wasn't pushing for the full story.

"Are you up to helping with a little construction?" Antony inserted. "I could use a second set of hands in there." He tilted his head toward the display room.

Bella beamed at him. "Sounds good." She paused and grabbed her phone out of her pocket, looking at the screen. After a moment, she smiled at them. "Hank is on his way. Looks like we might have even more help."

"You don't have to do that," Emory started, but Bella cut her off.

"We're family. It's what we do." Bella shrugged and walked toward Antony. "Better set that down somewhere," she said, pointing to the broken pieces. "Then we gotta get to work."

Antony looked at Emory, making sure she was okay with all of this, and she nodded at him. He sent her a little kiss, making her smile, and after dropping the broken display on the counter, headed into the display room.

"I'm almost done screwing the plywood onto the display," Antony said, walking over to where he'd stopped. "If you'll hold things in place, I think I can work a bit faster."

"Sounds good." Bella came over and helped him out for a few minutes in comfortable silence. But Antony should have known it was too good to be true. "Are you going to tell me what really happened?"

He paused, the screw dropping from his fingers. Scrambling to pick it up, he went to work, feigning nonchalance. "What are you talking about?"

Bella scoffed. "You really expect me to believe that her house just *happened* to break? Come on, Tony. I'm not an idiot."

He gave her a quick glare. "I never said you were."

"No, but you're treating me like one."

He sighed. "None of this is my story to tell," he said carefully.

"Maybe not, but we both know tight-lipped Emory won't share."

"Then I guess you have your answer."

Bella sighed. "Okay. I guess we'll have to do this the hard way."

Antony ignored her grumblings and went about his work. As he crawled out from under the display, he noticed Bella waiting for him. Antony raised his eyebrows in question.

"What if I might have news on your mother's ring?"

Antony's jaw dropped. "I thought Trisha sold it?"

Bella pursed her lips and smirked. "She did. But that doesn't mean there wasn't a trail."

"Then where is it?"

She held out her hand. "What's the story about Emory's house?"

"Extortion? Really?" Antony tilted her head and gave her a look.

Bella grinned. "That's a really nasty word." She narrowed her gaze. "Maybe just call it an incentive."

"You're willing to risk my relationship with your cousin," Antony pointed a finger at Bella, "which I had to work extra hard for, on a bit of information?"

Bella scrunched up her nose. "It sounds bad when you say it like that."

"Because it is!" Antony said, throwing his free hand in the air.

"Bella." A deep voice from the doorway broke into their conversation, and Antony spun around to see Detective Hank standing there, glaring.

"What?" she asked sweetly.

"Stop trying to blackmail people."

Bella put on a casual stance, studying her nail. "I don't know what you're talking about," she said easily.

The detective rubbed his forehead. "Must we go through this again?"

She put her hands behind her back and opened her eyes until they were wide and innocent-looking.

Antony had to give Bella credit. She knew how to work the crowd. If he hadn't seen her in action only moments before, he might actually believe her little act.

"Don't make me arrest you for interfering with an investigation," Detective Hank threatened.

She grinned and bounced on her toes. "Would I actually get to see the inside of a jail cell this time? I've never been in one! Ooh! Could I do an undercover story? You know, like from the inside?"

Antony bit his lips between his teeth. Bella was really going after what she wanted and it was clear that it was about to drive the detective crazy.

Detective Hank's face was turning a weird shade of red and his mouth was pinched tight. "Bella," he warned.

"Yes, Hank?"

The large man stormed toward her and Antony found himself backing up toward the kitchen door. He slipped away just as the detective reached Bella, but Antony found himself unconcerned when the smile never left her face. *If she's not afraid of him, then I won't worry about it either.*

"Everything okay?"

Antony turned and put a finger to his lips. "I do believe the detective is giving Bella a scolding."

Emory wiped her hands on a towel and slung it over her shoulder. "Wait...what?"

Antony grinned as she walked over to him. Again he put his finger to his lips, then cracked open the swinging door. He had to pinch his lips together as he tilted his head around just enough to see two entwined bodies.

He shooed Emory back into the kitchen when her jaw dropped open.

"Sorry," he said. "I didn't want you to make any noise and interrupt them."

Emory's mouth snapped up and down a few times. "You didn't want me to interrupt them?" She put her hands on her hips. "It looks to me like someone should interrupt them. That is definitely not a kiss fit for a public arena."

Antony chuckled and grabbed her around the waist, laughing harder when she struggled against him. "Let the man have his fun. I have a feeling Bella is going to lead him on a merry chase before this is all over."

"Whatever," Emory grumbled.

Antony sniffed the air. "Is your gingerbread in the oven?" he asked.

She nodded. "Yeah." She held up crossed fingers. "Here's hoping it bakes right so I can get started on it quickly."

"How long ago did you put it in?"

"Just a couple minutes ago. Why?" she asked with a frown.

"Because that gives us plenty of time for an indecent kiss of our own," Antony quipped before bringing his lips down to hers.

CHAPTER 11

E mory's hand felt as if it were going to fall off. She paused her work and flexed her fingers, the muscles screaming in resistance. "Come on," she grumbled to herself. "I'm only half-done. You can't give out now." She stared hard at her fingers, but they didn't answer her back. Sighing, she set down the bag of icing and forced herself to take a break.

Leaving the corner of the kitchen where she had set up shop in order to keep things more secret and safer, Emory wandered into the display room. She stopped to admire Antony and Enoch's work. Not to mention Bella and Hank's. It was magnificent! Warm lighting from the Christmas strands gave a homey, cozy glow to the room. Trees lined the walls, full of ribbons and gingerbread cookies.

The display tables were covered in cloth and lights, creating the look of snowy hills, yet leaving room for the train track, which was almost finished winding its way around the tables.

"Good thing, too," she mumbled to herself. "The doors open tomorrow for the competitors to bring their displays." There was a two-day window for everyone to bring their gingerbread houses to Gingerbread Inn. After that, there were two days of judging, and then, on Christmas Eve, the room was opened for visitors.

During the open house on Christmas Eve, the winners would be announced and the display would continue to be open for showings through the beginning of the year. The event had become an important one for Seagull Cove, as it drove tourists and guests to their tiny town during the usually quiet winter season. The stint of visitors might be short, but the pop in the economy for those couple of weeks were enough to help take the sting off six months of little to no business.

Emory hummed in satisfaction. She could do this. She would finish her gingerbread piece and everything would go off without a hitch. They might not have caught their food thief yet, and Mrs. Pearson might still have it out for first place, but Emory just knew that all her hard work was going to pay off. She was going to win, everyone would see that she wasn't some failure in the Simmons line, and her grandmother would be able to find pride in what her granddaughter was doing. "All it took was a bit of hard work," she murmured, massaging her still sore appendage.

"It looks so good!"

Emory turned and smiled. "Hey, Hope. How are you feeling?"

Hope's hand drifted to the stitches on her cheek and she grimaced. "Fine. I mean, I'm sore and stuff, but I'll be all right."

Emory walked over and wrapped her arm around her cousin's shoulders. "I'm just glad you caught Trisha. It still blows my mind that she was flat out stealing things, and all over a boy!"

Hope gave her a look. "He's a man, thank you very much."

Emory laughed softly. "I suppose he is," she said softly, her eyes going back to the room. "He sure did a good job in here."

Hope elbowed Emory. "Him and Antony, you mean. That *man* of yours isn't too bad either."

Emory smiled. "I suppose he's not."

"I don't know that I've ever seen you date someone," Hope said thoughtfully, then smiled. "I think it's been good for you. You smile much more than you used to."

Emory gave her cousin a dry look. "Gee, thanks."

"You know what I mean," Hope defended. "You've always been so...serious." She put her hand up to stop any arguments. "I'm not saying that's a bad thing, I'm simply stating facts." Hope's look was warm. "I've always loved you, no matter how stoic you were."

Emory smiled and turned away. If she wasn't careful, she would tear up at Hope's words. Being an only child had made Emory feel like she had to conquer the world. All her parents' time, energy, and money had gone into giving her the best of life. And now the weight of that responsibility sat heavily on Emory's shoulders. In Seattle, there had been little opportunity to prove herself. Now, however, she felt as if she might break under the expectations. But with the realization of the display room, things were feeling better.

"Antony has brought out your softer side," Hope continued. "And I think it's wonderful."

"Don't get too excited," Emory shot back. "I'm still hard on the inside."

"Liar."

Emory chuckled. "What can I say? I'm a softie at heart."

"Now that I believe," Hope said with a nod.

Emory sighed. "I'm sorry if I've been hard to get along with over the years. I just get so focused and don't always notice everything around me."

"It's a trait to be admired," Hope said lovingly. "There are plenty of people who can't focus to save their lives."

"And there are those of us who are so focused, we lose ours," Emory said sarcastically.

Hope laughed softly, then winced and touched her cheek. "No smiling that wide yet, apparently."

"You just now noticed that?" Emory clucked her tongue. "Enoch must not be doing his job." She looked at Hope, then burst out laughing. "Or maybe he's doing his job too well, huh?"

Hope shook her head, her cheeks fiery red. "You're terrible."

"I know." Emory wiped at her eyes. "But you're the one who reacted so strongly. I can't be held responsible for my response."

"Hope?"

The women turned around.

"Hey, Enoch!" Hope chirped, and Emory swallowed her laughter. Quiet, little Hope was certainly coming out of her shell around the good-looking handyman.

"Hey, sweetheart," he said, walking in to kiss her cheek. "I thought you were back to work today."

She shrugged. "I was, but I got distracted by Emory's display room."

Emory put her hands in the air. "It's not mine. Your boyfriend built it."

Enoch grinned. "Maybe we need to say *the* boyfriends built it. I'd have never finished if it weren't for Antony. He was a big help."

"I'm glad to hear it," Emory said, putting her hands on her hips.

"He ought to be good for something, right?" Antony's voice quipped, surprising everyone in the room.

"Speak of the devil," Emory said, smiling to soften her teasing.

Antony chuckled. "If, when you say devil, you mean handsome as sin, then yes...that's me."

"Oh my gosh." Emory groaned, slapping her forehead. "You can turn anything into a compliment."

Antony shrugged. "It's a gift."

Laughing, Enoch took Hope's hand. "Come on, babe. We don't want to get in the middle of this argument."

Emory shook her head, but smiled and waved as Hope and Enoch left. After they were gone, she turned to Antony. "What brings you here so early? Usually you're still baking at this time."

Antony stalked toward with an intense look and Emory held her breath. "Just needed to refill my sugar supply," he said before giving her a short but searing kiss.

"FEELING BETTER?" EMORY asked breathlessly after he pulled away, her eyes slowly fluttering open.

Antony couldn't help but smile that her eyes took longer to open than his. If anything was going to feed his ego, it was the fact that Emory was so affected by his touch. Was there a man who didn't take pride in knocking a woman off-balance by his kiss? *Not that I know of,* Antony mentally answered his own question. "Much," he said in response to her question. "How have you been today? Is the house about done?"

Emory scrunched up her nose. "It's coming. I think I'm going to make it though." She massaged her palm. "Much to my hand's dismay."

Antony reached out and took her sore hand, slowly massaging it while keeping eye contact. "I can't decorate for you, but I can help with this."

Emory blew out a long breath. "Do you always know what to say?"

"Eh...it's a gift."

Emory laughed. "Another one? You're so ridiculous."

Wrapping his arm around her shoulders, he kissed her temple. "As long as it keeps you laughing, being ridiculous is worth it."

"I should get back to work," she said with a sigh, then peered up at him. "Although, you didn't tell me why you were here so early."

"Business has been slow. I didn't need to make as many things this morning."

Emory frowned. "I'm sorry. Slower than the normal winter crowd? Or just slow because it *is* the winter crowd?"

Antony shrugged and settled himself on a bar stool. "This is my first winter, so it's hard to tell."

Emory paused, then turned away from her project and folded her arms over her chest. "What aren't you telling me?"

Antony grinned. "That my sugar supply isn't full yet?"

He could practically see the blush creep up her neck. "Stop trying to distract me," she grumbled, giving him a scolding look. "I can tell something's going on. What is it?"

Antony tapped his finger on the counter top for a moment before answering. "I think Mrs. Pearson is messing with my business."

"What?" Emory screeched. Antony winced at the shrillness of the tone and fought the need to cover his ears.

"I don't know anything for sure," he said. "It's all just conjecture."

Emory walked over and put her palms on the counter, leaning in. "Tell me everything that has happened."

Antony's eyebrows shot up. "Wait a minute, who's protecting who here?" he teased. "I'm struggling to feel like I'm wearing the pants in this relationship."

"When we both wear aprons, I think that's a moot point," she shot back, making Antony laugh.

"True enough." He took in a deep breath. "Like I said, I'm not sure of anything at the moment, so I'm not going to do anything just yet."

"I still want to know what's going on," she pressed, her blue eyes sad and begging.

"Geez." He reached across the counter to caress her cheek. "You could win a war with those baby blues."

Emory shook her head. "You're doing it again."

He slapped his hands on the counter. "Fine, fine." Antony blew out a long breath. "I think someone is pureposefully keeping my regular customers away."

Emory's jaw dropped. "You've got to be kidding me."

"I wish," Antony grumbled. It had been bothering him all morning, when his normal rush of regulars didn't grab their pastries to go with their morning coffee. After stepping outside to double check that the door was unlocked, he'd watched a few people walk past, their eyes downcast, unwilling to speak to him or come in.

"What are you going to do about it?"

"What can I do?" Antony argued. "I don't know who's doing it."

"Don't you have security cameras?"

Antony frowned. "No. I can't afford them yet."

"We should talk to your neighbors. They probably do."

Antony nodded. "That sounds like a good plan. Maybe Hank will have something to say about it as well." Antony looked around. "I'm sure I'll eventually see him, as long as Bella's around."

"I hope he's off doing his job," Emory said. "We need to figure out who's been stealing my food." She pursed her lips. "And Bella needs to do her job."

Antony snorted.

Emory turned back to her work. Antony pulled out his phone, scrolling down his social media, content to just be with her at the moment. It was far more peaceful than continuing to freak out about why no one wanted to come to his bakery. A flash of guilt hit him as he realized he'd left Jennifer to handle all that, but he brushed it off. *It's not like it's hard work. She'll be fine. Plus I told her to call the police if she saw anything.*

Emory gasped. "Not again!"

Antony looked up. "What?"

"My bag of sour apples is missing!"

Antony stood from the stool, stuffing his phone in his back pocket. "You think the thief took it?"

"Who else?" Emory demanded. "They were here when I was working earlier." She growled softly. "I took a break because my hand was hurting, and Hope and I chatted for awhile." Emory spun around, her face red and her eyes misty. "What the heck is going on, Antony? I know we caught the jewelry thief, but there are still so many weird things going on! I feel like we're being targeted."

Antony sighed and pulled her against his chest. The little thrill he got every time she leaned into him still shot through his system, but it wasn't as happy as it normally was. It was tainted by the feeling that Emory was right. It definitely felt like they were being targeted. *But why? What are they hoping to gain?*

Sniffling, Emory raised her head and looked him in the eye. "I'm done being a victim," she said darkly. "I want this finished."

"Okay..." Antony said warily. "What are you planning to do?"

Pushing off his chest, she started to march out of the kitchen. "The first thing I'm going to do is head up to that hidden attic Enoch mentioned. You know, the one where they found my pie plate?"

Antony nodded.

"After the announcement, Bella explored it with Hank, but I never went inside," Emory pressed.

Antony lunged after her, grabbing her arm. "Wait a second. If you think I'm letting you go alone, you're loopy."

She glared at him. "Well, then, come on. Because I'm going now."

Antony straightened his shirt. "Do you even know where you're going?"

She shook her head. "No. But I'm sure I'll figure it out." She began walking again. "After all, how many hidden attics can there be in this place?"

"How many, indeed?" Antony grumbled, hurrying after her. He snatched a meat tenderizer on his way out the kitchen door and tucked it in his back pocket. *Just in case...*

CHAPTER 12

E mory wasn't about to admit it, but hearing Antony's footsteps behind her was a relief. As frustrated as she was, she really didn't want to go wandering through the belly of the huge mansion by herself. In the dark. Not knowing where she was going. *Antony won't know either, but at least I won't be alone.*

She headed into the laundry room and began to scan the walls. "Enoch said it was around here somewhere," she muttered to herself.

"Looking for this?"

Emory turned around to see Antony holding a slightly open doorway. She scrunched her nose. "It's tiny. How in the world did Enoch get through there?"

Antony shrugged. "Yeah...it's gonna be a tight fit, for sure." He stuck his head inside, then came back out. "Do you have a flashlight? It's pitch black in there."

Emory nodded and reached for the cupboard above the washer. Her grandmother always kept emergency supplies on hand. Grabbing the biggest one she could find, Emory walked over to the doorway and turned it on. The bright light lit up the dust and spiderwebs that seemed to infiltrate every corner of the space. "Ew," she whined, swiping a stray web out of her face. "This is going to be gross."

"Nothing like your pristine kitchen," Antony said from behind her. "Want me to go first so I can break the line?"

Emory only hesitated for a second. "No thanks. I started this, I should lead."

"Yes, ma'am," Antony teased.

Emory huffed through her nose and almost smiled, but her heart was pounding so hard, and fear of what she might find was trying to claw its way up her throat, to the point that she struggled to find humor in the joke. Taking a deep breath, she stepped into the dark and began to march ahead.

For the first few moments, only the sound of her breathing broke the silence. Emory tried to control how loud she was being, but there was nothing for it. She gulped hard and gave up trying to keep her chest moving normally. *I'm scared. That's all there is to it. But I can still do this. If I work hard enough, I can conquer anything.*

A loud groan burst through the air and Emory squeaked, leaping backward only to scream when she hit a body.

"Easy, Em," Antony said, bringing his arms around her. "It's just me."

"I'm sorry." She gasped, putting her hands on her knees. "I'm completely freaked out, and that noise made me forget you were there."

Antony chuckled and rubbed her back. "If I was anyone else, that would be really hard on my pride," he teased.

Emory laughed a little through her panting. "Truer words have never been spoken." She straightened herself and brushed down her apron. "Okay. Old houses make scary noises. It's just the wind." She shone the light around and paused. "There!"

"What?" Antony stepped up close behind her.

"The stairs. Enoch said we have to go up them in order to get to the attic."

"You sure you want to do this?"

Emory nodded firmly, her determination winning over the fear. "Yes. We've got to figure this out."

"Okay. I'm with you."

Emory reached behind her and grabbed his hand, giving it a tight squeeze. "Thank you."

"Always."

That single word warmed Emory's fear and continued to swirl through her head as she cautiously began to go up the stairs. Images flashed through her head of Antony grinning from underneath the table when he was building the gingerbread display. His laughter as they decorated their Christmas cookies with silly designs. The heat of his gaze when he looked at her lips before taking her breath away with his kiss. The happiness she found every time she felt her phone buzz, knowing it had to be a text from him. The craving she felt for his company every time they had to say goodnight. The realization came hard, but wasn't as frightening as Emory expected it to be.

I love him.

She bit her lip at the thought. *I love him. I don't know how I let it happen, but I do.* She peered discreetly behind herself as they walked along the small hallway. "Oof!" Emory cursed mentally and rubbed the side of her head.

"Are you okay?" Antony grabbed her shoulders and spun her around. She could barely see his face in the darkness—only a little light from their flashlights was landing on him—but the sharp lines of his cheekbones and concerned look in those gray eyes were almost more than she could handle.

"Uh...yeah," she mumbled. *Oh my gosh. Watch where you're going, Emory! I can't believe I ran into a wall.* She shook herself and turned forward again, shaking off his hold. There was something stronger than normal about his touch now that she knew her feelings. *But right now is NOT the time to bring it up,* she scolded herself. *You're in the middle of a secret passageway, can barely see where you're going, and have no idea what's ahead. Put your game face on and focus.*

ANTONY GRINNED AND shook his head as she took off again. He had no idea why she'd run into a wall, but he was equal parts worried and amused. The light in her hand still trembled slightly, letting him know that she was scared, but nothing seemed to be able to hold back his Emory.

The possessive word in his thoughts caught him off-guard. There was something decidedly...permanent about thinking of her as *his*. Antony snorted, pushing the weird thoughts to the side. Right now wasn't the time to be examining his inner thoughts.

A thud brought them both to a halt and Antony's heart beat faster. He had to fight the urge to pull Emory behind him. He wanted to protect her, but she wasn't one to hide. Her determination and grit were a characteristic he adored and treating her like a fragile woman would go completely against that. Instead, he held himself at the ready, but stayed in the back.

Footsteps thundered nearby and Antony whirled in a circle. He couldn't tell if the noise was coming from inside the walls or out. "Where are they?" he asked quietly.

Emory shook her head. "I don't know." Her jaw clenched hard in the dim light. "But they're getting closer."

She was right. The footsteps were quickly moving in their direction. "Turn off the light," Antony whispered. He turned off his own flashlight.

"Why?"

"Because if they're in our hallway, they'll run into us. But our lights will give us away otherwise."

Emory followed directions and they were plunged into the dark. The groaning of the house was still creating odd noises, but footsteps continued.

"Almost here," Antony murmured. He turned to the direction of the noise. The footsteps grew rapid, as if the person was coming down a set of stairs, and a small light began to bounce off the wooden walls around them. Antony couldn't fight the impulse any longer. He stepped forward and swapped places with Emory. They were about to meet a criminal and he didn't want her hurt. He ignored her hiss and blocked the walkway.

The small light moved closer until it stopped, then bounced up into Antony's eyes. He squinted and put his hands up to block it. "Crap," he muttered when the footsteps suddenly rushed in the other direction. Something that sounded like marbles hit the floor and the footsteps grew softer.

"He's getting away!" Emory shouted.

Antony lunged forward, following the sound as best he could. He switched his flashlight back on just as he stepped on something and lost his balance. Cursing under his breath, he fell, slamming his shoulder into the floor. Pain ricocheted through his neck and down his spine.

"Oh my gosh, Antony!" Emory landed at his side. "Are you okay?"

"Fine," he snapped. He scrambled to his feet, brushing off her concerned hands. Whatever was going on here was starting to tick him off.

"What happened?"

Antony squatted and felt around until he found his flashlight, then finished turning it on. "I tripped on something." He pointed the light toward the floor and picked up something green. Sighing, he rose and held it out to Emory. "Look familiar?"

Her eyes widened in the shadows. "It's my candy!"

Antony nodded and looked behind him. "And whoever had them is long gone by now." He ground his jaw. While he'd believed Emory when she said someone was taking her food, Antony had figured there was a logical explanation for it. Perhaps one of the guests felt they had a right to whatever they wanted, or something like that. After all, what were the odds that they had two thieves running around the mansion?

"We were so close," Emory whispered. "How will we ever catch them now?"

Antony deflated and hung his head. "I'm sorry."

A small hand landed on his back. "This isn't your fault, Antony," she said softly. "I'm the one who came bursting in here unprepared."

Antony shook his head. "If I hadn't pushed you out of the way and run, we might have had a chance to catch them."

Emory shook her head hard. "No. That light was blinding and they had the advantage, since the light was facing away from them. They were still in the dark."

He blew out a long breath and pushed a hand through his hair. "Why don't we try to see where they were coming from, huh? Maybe we'll find some clues."

Emory nodded. "Sounds good."

Antony faced the way the intruder had run and reached one hand back. When Emory took it and held tight, it made him feel slightly better, but his pride still rankled over being bested by a small piece of candy. Those candies were crunching under his boots as they walked along for a few feet.

"Apparently they hadn't gotten around to eating them yet," Emory said sarcastically.

Antony didn't say anything. He was searching high and low for a reason that the person had sounded like they were coming downstairs. "There," he murmured.

"What?" Emory stepped up close and leaned around him. "What did you find?"

"Stairs," he answered. "I'm guessing they lead to the attic Enoch talked about." He heard Emory take a deep breath.

"Okay, then. At least that means it's the same person, right?"

"Should be," Antony murmured in return, distracted as he searched for more clues. "I can't imagine we have a family living up here and no one knows about it."

"I have to admit I'm surprised they came back," Emory continued. "After Enoch found the spot, Hank came up here and did a thorough search. Why didn't they run when their stuff was taken away?"

"Maybe they figured it was a one-time thing." Antony let go of Emory's hand and began to walk carefully up the stairs. The groaning beneath his feet mingled with the wind whipping outside, and he worried that he was too large to be stepping on the planks. *Hank is bigger than you,* he reminded himself. *Surely it'll be fine.*

When they got to the top, the door was shut and Antony wasted no time in throwing it open. The thief wasn't here anyway. Stepping boldly inside, he shone his light around. "This can't be a pleasant place to stay," he murmured. Cobwebs, dirt, and garbage seemed to fill the corners of the space, though a slightly broken table took up the middle. The slanting ceiling made moving around difficult, but the window in the far wall helped illuminate the space a little.

"I just don't get it," Emory whispered. "Why would someone stay here? Do you think they're homeless? Or maybe mentally unstable?"

Antony shook his head. "I don't know. But something isn't right."

They looked around for a few more minutes, but didn't find anything useful. Detective Hank had taken most of the items when he'd searched previously.

"There's nothing here," Emory said with a disappointed sigh. "Let's go back down."

Antony nodded. "Yeah...I think you're right." He held out his hand and began to lead her back down the stairs.

As they crunched over the spilled candy, Emory grumbled something about coming back with a broom.

Antony shifted his bruised shoulder as he relived the fall. He was pretty sure it would look black and blue when he studied it in the mirror later. A few minutes later, they emerged from the tunnels, both dirty and exhausted.

"I never knew fear was so tiring," Emory said, blowing her hair out of her face.

Antony chuckled and brushed aside the loose strand. "It's the adrenaline. When it goes down, so does your energy. Maybe you should take a nap?" He gave her a look. "I'll be your pillow."

Emory laughed and shook her head. "I need to clean up and get back to work. That wall still needs a little—"

A scream caused them both to jump.

"What was that?" Emory asked breathlessly.

Antony didn't answer. He was too busy running into the hallway, determined to end it this time, once and for all.

CHAPTER 13

E mory ran after Antony. That scream was definitely someone who was scared, but the weirdest part was, it sounded like someone young. *We don't have any kids staying at the inn. Who the heck could it be?* She skidded to a stop just after passing the door to the gingerbread room.

"Please, no," she whispered, hoping her ears and eyes were deceiving her. Before stepping to the doorway, she closed her eyes, and sure enough...someone was quietly crying. When she opened them again, a crowd was coming down the hallway, covering the crying noise with their own shouts of concerns.

Emory put up her hand and the group stopped.

"What?" Bella asked, putting her hands on her hips and tapping her foot. "What happened?"

Emory shook her head, not daring to speak. She stepped backward until she was in the doorway and slowly pivoted. Her heart sunk to the floor. Almost every part of the display was destroyed. Single tables had been turned over. The connected ones with the train had been smashed by falling Christmas trees.

And there, in the back of the destruction, Antony was squatted down, peering under some of the wreckage. Now that everyone had quieted down, Emory was sure that the crying she was hearing was coming from that spot, and Antony's warm, soft tones were blending over the noise.

"What is going on?" Bella hissed, coming up right behind Emory.

Emory looked over her shoulder. "I think everyone should stay back."

Hank was right behind Bella. "Let me in, Emory."

Reluctantly, she stepped aside, then changed her mind and darted into the room, hurrying to Antony's side. There was something about his posture that let her know the situation wasn't dangerous; however, she still was insanely curious about who Antony had found. After kneeling, she put a hand on Antony's back and leaned down, only to gasp. "It's a boy!"

The young boy scowled at her. His red, dirty face was covered in tears and scum. It looked like he hadn't showered in days and Emory's sensitive nose caught the scent of body odor, only verifying her suspicions.

"Em," Antony said carefully, "this is Jim. Jim Harmon." He turned his gray eyes to hers. "I think we've found our hungry thief."

At those words, the boy, who appeared to be around twelve years old, began to cry again. The tears trickled down his cheeks and his bottom lip trembled.

"Emory, what's going on under there?"

Emory looked over her shoulder to see Hank looking impatient. She sighed and pushed off Antony in order to stand. "Antony thinks he caught our thief."

Antony scooted to the side and Hank got down on his knees, pushing his baseball hat back with his thumb. "What do we have here?" he asked, tilting his head in a curious manner. "Mind telling me your name, son?"

"I'm not your son," the boy said angrily.

Bella threaded her arm through Emory's as they watched Hank interact with the intruder.

"That might be, but I'd still like to know your name."

There was a long pause before he finally answered. "Jim. And I already told that guy."

Emory could only assume the boy was pointing to Antony. Hank looked up and Antony nodded, before Hank focused on the child again. "Can you tell me where your parents are?"

"I don't have any."

Bella gasped and Emory felt her jaw slacken. "No parents?" she whispered. "How's that possible?"

"Everyone has parents, Jim, even if they don't like them," Hank said easily.

"Not everyone. Orphans don't have parents."

"Are you an orphan?"

The boy didn't talk anymore and Emory knew that was his answer. Her heart, which was already aching from the disaster of the gingerbread room, felt like it literally broke in two.

Bella, however, was not frozen in her grief. She got on the floor and began to crawl toward Jim.

"Bella," Hank warned, his voice growing testy.

"Lay off, big guy," she snipped back. "This guy needs a hug, and I aim to give it to him." Emory watched her cousin disappear into the wreckage, despite Hank's protests. There was a murmur of voices, and then Hank backed up and stood on his feet.

"I'm gonna kill her," he muttered, rubbing the edge of his jaw so hard Emory was sure the skin was going to be raw.

"And I thought you were stubborn," Antony said quietly, having come around to stand by Emory.

Emory elbowed him in the ribs. "Watch it," she teased, though her thoughts weren't on their flirting. She was too busy watching Bella crawl out with Jim at her heels.

"Emory?"

She raised her eyebrows in question.

"Jim here needs a cookie and a glass of milk." Bella smiled down at the boy, her arm around his thin shoulders. "Think you can help us out?"

Emory studied the boy. The large, black, oversized sweatshirt he was wearing nearly hit his knees. It was stained and torn in places, and the jeans he was wearing were too short, leaving his ankles bare. The skin looked chapped from the cold and his shoes were in no better shape than the rest of his clothing. He made such a pitiful picture that all the anger she'd had about her stolen food slipped away. She shook her head. "No..." she started, causing Bella to shoot her a look. "I actually don't have any warm cookies at the moment." She smiled. "But I do have some scones. They're chocolate chip," she added, hoping that was enticing enough.

The boy frowned. "What's a scone?"

"You've never had a scone?" Bella asked, aghast. She put a hand on her chest and began to walk the boy toward the kitchen door. "They're only the best things ever!" She bent a little lower to his level. "They're like a mix between a biscuit and cookie." Her voice trailed off as they disappeared into the kitchen.

The rest of the room was quiet, no one quite sure what to say after that.

Emory turned a full circle, her eyes refilling with tears. She shook her head. It was ruined. All of it was ruined. The competition would have to be cancelled and she would go down as a failure in the Simmons family.

Antony's hands landed on her shoulders. "Don't worry," he said. "We'll fix it."

Emory shook her head harder and wiped at her eyes. "It doesn't matter," she said with false bravado. It did matter. It mattered to her. But how could she be so selfish in the face of a homeless, hungry little boy? Turning, she marched toward the kitchen. "Right now we need to take care of a little boy and finally get to the bottom of it all."

ANTONY WATCHED EMORY walk away with her head held high, and the admiration in him soared.

"She's quite something," Hank said, coming to Antony's side.

Antony nodded. "She is."

"And a bit less stubborn than her cousin," Hank grumbled.

Antony chuckled and stuffed his hands in his pockets. "I doubt it," he said. "She just might be less...prone to waving it in people's faces."

Hank continued to grumble while the two men walked into the kitchen to find all three cousins and Grandma Claire gushing over the boy.

Jim had a smirk on his face while the women doted on him, plus a plate with a sandwich, some apple slices, and the promised scone.

"I think he eats better than I do," Hank quipped, folding his arms over his broad chest.

All the women looked his way with varying degrees of surprise. "If you'd barely been eating enough to live on for the last four months, you might get a good meal and some sympathy too," Bella sniffed. She ran a hand over the boy's head, smiling at him. "Fill your belly and then we'll get you all cleaned up, okay?"

"Now, hold on," Hank said, grabbing a chair and turning it backward so he could straddle it. He sat down across from the child. "We need to have a chat," he stated firmly, but not unkindly.

Antony agreed with Hank, and moved to stand close behind the detective so the boy knew they meant business. Jim had been a frightened, shaking mess when Antony had found him in the corner. He was sobbing loudly, muttering something about how he didn't do it. His entire body had been trembling and the smell of him was enough to knock Antony on his backside. He'd managed to get Jim to talk to him, but that's as far as it had gone before the crowd had interrupted.

The boy had obviously been neglected, and from the green stickiness of his hands, Antony knew they'd found their attic ghost. But the question was, why? Why was this boy living in the attic? Where was his family, and how did he get here?

"Careful, Hank," Bella warned. Every woman there had a resolved look on her face, and it was easy to see that they were going into 'protective mama' mode. Antony held back his grin. He didn't envy Hank's position, though he did agree with it.

"I have to do my job, Bell," he said. "That's what I'm here for."

She sighed. "I know, but just...go easy on him, huh?"

Hank nodded.

He'd never struck Antony as cruel, so Antony wasn't worried. He just wanted to get this over with.

"Jim," Hank said, securing the boy's attention. "I need to know how long you've been at the inn."

Jim scrunched his eyebrows. "Inn?"

"This house," Emory clarified. "It's called Gingerbread Inn."

Jim's face lit up. "Is that why you made that beautiful gingerbread house? Because this is the Gingerbread Inn?"

Antony watched Emory's face fall, but she nodded anyway. "Yeah, that's part of it." He knew how much the reminder of the festival must pain her. Carrying on her grandmother's tradition was everything to her. Antony's heart ached, and he made a mental note to comfort her later.

Jim shrugged and took a large bite of his sandwich. "I've been here a few months, I guess." He glanced at Bella, then to Hank. "I got here in August."

Antony's eyes widened and he looked to Emory, who simply looked resigned. "Five months?" he mouthed, holding up that many fingers.

She pursed her lips and nodded.

"How did you get here?" Hank asked.

"Walked."

Antony frowned.

"Walked? From where?"

Jim's eyes went to his plate. "Nowhere."

"Now, Jim, that's not going to cut it," Hank said. "I don't want to be the bad guy here, but I need some answers. We've had quite a bit of food disappear here at the inn, and some other problems as well, and I'm guessing you have something to do with it all."

Jim's eyes widened and he swallowed hard, slinking back in his seat, slowly shaking his head.

"Now the display room for the gingerbread competition has been ruined, and who did we find cowering in the corner?"

"Hank!" Bella scolded.

Jim's head shook harder and the tears from earlier started to come back. Antony found himself feeling bad for the boy, but he knew they needed answers. "Jim," he said softly, pulling the boy's brown eyes to him. "No one wants to hurt you," Antony said softly, as if addressing a wild colt. "We want to help. But we need the whole story." He tilted his head. "Can you please give that to us?"

"Why is no one around in this inn when you need—" Antony's mother came storming into the room and abruptly stopped.

Antony groaned quietly and pinched the bridge of his nose. All they needed was his dramatic mother.

"What's going on here?" she demanded.

"Look, Mrs. Harrison," Hank said, standing. "I'm on official business at the moment. So if you don't mind going out—"

"I will not leave," she stated firmly, walking further into the room. She narrowed her eyes at Jim. "What are you doing with this...ruffian?"

"Mother..." Antony intervened. "Now is not the time."

Jim's frightened eyes were darting from one person to the other as they talked over his head and Antony became afraid that the small boy might bolt.

"Lucia," Claire said, rising. "Let me walk you to the sitting room."

"Not this time, Claire," Antony's mother stated again. "I want to know what's going on." She looked at everyone in the room. "Is this the food thief?"

Antony reluctantly nodded when her eyes hit his.

She looked back to Jim. "How old are you?"

Jim's skinny chest rose and fell rapidly. "Twelve," he squeaked.

She nodded with resolve and came to sit at the table as close to Jim as she could get, then folded her hands on the table top. Her cool eyes met Detective Hank's. "You may proceed," she said. "But when this is done, I will be feeding him until he has a little meat on his bones." She turned to Jim. "Tell the detective what he needs to know."

Her matter-of-fact voice must have been exactly what Jim needed, because he opened his mouth and spilled a long, sad story.

CHAPTER 14

Go, Mama! Emory found herself rooting for the no-nonsense Italian mother, who planted herself at the kitchen table. Apparently, Jim also knew what was what because he launched right into his story and as he spoke, Emory's heart broke even more, though she'd have never believed it possible..

"My mom and dad are dead," he said baldly.

Almost every adult in the room shifted in some way, as if the information made them uncomfortable.

"When did they die?" Hank asked.

"When I was a kid," Jim said. His eyes fell to his lap.

"When, Jim?"

"When I was nine."

Hank nodded and made a note in his phone. "Go on. Where have you been staying all this time?"

He glared up at Hank. "Lots of different houses."

"Are you in the foster care system?"

Jim nodded, his body slumping in his chair. "But I don't like it there. The moms don't make cookies...or scones." He peeked up at Emory and she smiled at him encouragingly, though she knew her heart wasn't in it. "They don't read stories or throw a ball either." He sighed. "Until I stayed with Ms. Eugene."

"When did you stay with her?" Hank asked, still taking notes.

"I don't know, it was earlier this year."

"Go on. What happened?"

"The lady took me away again. Said Ms. Eugene was sick." Jim's bottom lip began to quiver. "I know she's old, but she would smile at me and say nice things. I liked the way she would pop popcorn and we watched movies together."

Bella put her hand on the boy's shoulder, giving it a squeeze.

"What happened with the next people?" Hank pressed.

"They were just like all the others," Jim said bitterly. "No one would talk to me or pay attention. They always told me to go do something else." He scoffed. "Like I'm some small kid who'll just sit and play with toys."

"So what did you do?"

Jim shrugged, his eyes drifting to Mrs. Harrison, who gave him a look. "I ran away," he finally stated. "I was sick of it all."

Hank nodded. "And how did you get here?"

"I kept to the woods and just kept going. Eventually I found this place." He picked at his jacket. "At first I tried staying in the garage, but somebody lives there and I almost got caught a couple of times."

"Enoch," Hope whispered. "He said someone had been messing with his tools."

Jim nodded. "Yeah. I thought they were interesting. My dad used to build things."

"What next?" Hank encouraged.

"When I knew I couldn't stay in the garage, I was walking around the house and found a small door in the back. That led me to the attic." Jim kept his head down, refusing to look anyone in the eye. His hair was too long and covered half of his face, only adding to the unkempt look he was sporting. "It was warmer up there and the wind couldn't get to me." He scrunched up his nose. "You guys have a mouse problem. Did you know that? They're everywhere upstairs."

Emory bit back a smile when Hope squeaked.

"The house is a hundred years old," Grandma Claire said firmly. She gave him a look. "You're lucky that's all that was up there."

Jim rolled his eyes. "I'm not scared of ghosts. I'm not a kid anymore."

Grandma clicked her tongue, but didn't speak more.

"Have you been stealing food?" Hank asked.

Jim's head sunk back down to his chest. "Yeah. I was hungry and there was so much that I figured no one would care."

"Henry," Grandma Claire said. "Under the circumstances, I think the boy needs to stay here."

Hank's eyebrows shot up just as another person shot into the room.

"Claire?" Sheriff Davidson bellowed. "What in the name of sam hill is going on?"

"Calm down, William, or you'll burst a blood vessel," Grandma Claire scolded.

He tore his hat off his head. "Forgive me," he snapped back. "But when I get a text saying I'm needed, my first thought is that someone is in trouble." He bent over, breathing heavily. "Had to put on the lights and everything to get out here between all the traffic on Main."

Antony started to laugh, but Emory sent him a scathing look, and he swallowed it back, but his eyes were still twinkling with that familiar light.

Emory felt her heart flutter in response and her neck started to heat up. She cleared her throat and turned back to the fight going on between Grandma and the sheriff.

Finally, Mrs. Harrison stood. "Come," she said to Jim. "You will help me make pasta."

Emory watched the woman take Jim by the shoulders and lead him into the kitchen. They began opening cupboards until they found the pots and ingredients they needed.

"What the…" Bella stood next to Emory, watching in awe. "I can't believe it. There is a soft side to the drama queen." She looked over and smiled. "No offense, Antony."

"None taken," he said from Emory's side.

She looked up at him. "She said it, not me."

Antony gave her a crooked grin and slipped an arm around her waist before kissing her temple. "It's fine. I know Mother has a passionate side. But she's also a good mother. I mean, she raised seven children. She knows what she's doing."

"Seven?" Emory gasped. "You never told me that."

His grin widened.

"Let me guess...you're the youngest," Bella added.

Antony laughed. "Guilty as charged."

"Speaking of guilty," Hank said, standing up and joining in their little pow-wow. "I don't know what to do with the kid." He shook his head. "I'll have to call the social worker in charge of him, but I'm not sure how to handle the stealing."

"I don't want to press charges," Emory said quickly.

Hank raised an eyebrow. "None?"

Emory shook her head. Her heart went out to the boy. While she didn't condone his methods, she couldn't imagine what it was like to lose your love and support system. He was young and desperate. Stealing food to feed himself wasn't all that bad in the long run. *The display room, on the other hand...* She sighed and tears blurred her vision for what seemed the thousandth time. "But if you guys could help me cancel the gingerbread festival, I could certainly use help there."

BELLA SNORTED AND WRAPPED her arms around Emory. "Hang in there, hon. It'll turn out okay."

When Emory nodded and wiped at a slow-moving tear, Antony couldn't help himself anymore. He turned her into his chest and hugged her close. "I'm so sorry," he said. "I know you put your heart and soul into this."

She nodded against his sternum and he could hear her sniffling. "It's just a dumb festival," she said thickly. "It'll be okay."

Antony pushed her back and cupped her face, using his thumbs to wipe her tears. "I don't think we need to give up quite yet. Maybe instead of helping you cancel, we could help you rebuild."

"I should go get Enoch," Hope said from behind them, then rushed from the room.

"No, don't..." Emory deflated against Antony. "Rebuilding it would take all night. There's no way I can ask you guys to do that."

"You're not asking," Bella said primly. "We're offering." She turned a sweet smile to the detective. "Aren't we, Hank?"

Hank's eyebrows went up. "You sure you want me with a hammer? While I'm happy to pitch in somewhere, I'm pretty sure I'll only end up with bruised thumbs if I try to build something."

Antony chuckled, while Emory laughed lightly.

Bella tapped her bottom lip. "I've always had a thing for a man in a tool belt. Maybe I should go help Hope find Enoch."

Hank growled. "Really? That's how you want to play this?"

Bella's blue eyes were wide and innocent. "Play what? This isn't a game."

Hank rolled his eyes and huffed. "You, woman, are impossible."

"Thank you!" Bella chirped. She latched onto his arm and jumped in order to give him a kiss on the cheek. "I'll make sure it's worth your time," she whispered just loud enough for Antony and Emory to hear.

Antony cleared his throat and stepped back. "That might have been more info than I wanted."

Emory shook her head and palmed her forehead. "Ditto."

"Detective?" Antony's mother called out. "I think we've made a decision."

The group looked to where his mother, Mrs. Simmons, Sheriff Davidson, and Jim were still in the kitchen.

"And what's that?" Hank asked, his hand on Bella's lower back.

"Jim will stay here," Mrs. Simmons announced, giving them all a look as if she planned to quell any resistance. "At least until the proper authorities can be found. During that time, he will work with Enoch on the property to repay for the food he ate."

"What about the display room?" Hank asked, letting go of Bella and folding his arms over his chest. "That was a lot of property damage."

Jim's eyes grew wide and his already pale face grew ashen. "I didn't do it!" he cried, moving to rush from the kitchen. Sheriff Davidson stopped the boy before he got very far.

"Calm down, son," he said. "Calm down. No one here is going to hurt you."

Bella rushed over, but Antony kept his arms around Emory. "What do you mean, you didn't do it?" Bella asked quickly as she ran over. "You were in the middle of the whole thing."

Jim was shaking slightly and Antony watched his mother put her hand on his shoulder. The touch seemed to be enough to calm him and Jim spoke again. "I was running away from..." His eyes came to Antony. "Him." Jim pointed. "He was in the walls and surprised me."

Antony nodded, letting the boy know he understood.

"When I got downstairs, I came out through the laundry room and was going to head outside." His face crumpled. "I came into the gingerbread room and a man was in there hitting everything with a sledge hammer." His bottom lip began to shake. "He must have heard me come in, because he turned to me and raised the hammer over his head." Jim wiped his face on his sleeves. "I-I screamed and ran. I knew I couldn't run back into the hall, because I was afraid I would get caught. Instead, I crawled under one of the tables."

"No," Emory breathed. "Are you telling me that we still have another mystery person running around out there?"

Antony gave her a small squeeze. "Are you sure it was a man? It couldn't have been a woman?"

Emory spun and looked at him with an open jaw. "You think Mrs. Pearson had something to do with this?"

Antony shrugged. "I don't know, but at this point I wouldn't put anything past her."

"Has she given you a reason to think that?" Sheriff Davidson asked, his head tilted and eyes narrow.

Antony regretted saying anything, but he wasn't sure how to get out of it now. "I don't know. She was here the other day, knocked over Emory's house, and made some really rude remarks. This morning, I had almost no customers, which is very unusual."

Sheriff Davidson sighed and scratched the side of his head. "Sounds like we need to have a chat."

"That's not important now," Antony said. "I knew it was a long shot. I mean, there's no way Mrs. Pearson could swing a sledgehammer, but I wanted to make sure."

Everyone turned back to Jim, who shook his head. "This guy was tall, and it was definitely a guy."

"Did you see his face?"

Jim scrunched his nose. "Only a little. He was wearing a black hood."

"Have you ever seen him before?" Bella pressed, her eyes gleaming in excitement.

"I think she's enjoying this," Emory said with a resigned chuckle.

Antony nodded his agreement.

"No," Jim finished. "He ran out when I climbed under the table. I think he was afraid other people heard me yell."

Hank tucked his phone back in his pocket. "Guess I'm sticking around Seagull Cove a little longer," he murmured.

There was no mistaking the relief in Bella's face at Hank's remark.

"Okay..." Antony said, stepping in. "Since it doesn't sound like Jim can help us any more right now, some of us have a project to get to."

"You really think we can get it back up?" Emory asked. Her eyes were wide and trusting, and Antony felt another surge of that feeling he'd had when they were behind the walls. It felt suspiciously more permanent than the strong interest he'd started this relationship with.

Nodding slowly, he kept eye contact. "I do."

Emory blinked several times, her eyes slightly misty, then swallowed. "Okay." She took a deep breath. "If you really think we can do this, then I believe you."

Antony tucked her into his chest, putting his chin on the top of her head. "You'll see. With this many people behind you, we can fix anything." *And maybe by the end of it all, you'll realize that I'm falling in love with you.*

CHAPTER 15

E mory rubbed at her eyes. They were tired, gritty, and her entire body ached. The sounds of electric drills came to a stop and Bella bounced to her feet.

"I think that's it!" she cried out.

"Is it really?" Emory blinked, trying to clear her vision. As she looked around, she realized the windows were bright. They'd worked the whole night through. "Oh!" she squeaked when strong arms came around her waist, only relaxing when she realized it was Antony.

"You did it," he whispered into her ear, then kissed the edge.

"We did it," she whispered back. "I couldn't have done this without you. I can't believe you all would stay here like this."

Antony turned her around. His eyes were tired, but his smile warmed her clear to her core, as usual. "You know why everyone stayed, right?"

Emory frowned a little and tilted her head. "What do you mean?"

He leaned down and brought their foreheads together, taking a deep breath as if breathing her in. "Everyone is here, Emory, because they love you."

Emory froze. *Wait...* "Antony..." she breathed.

"I love you, Emory," he continued. "I was drawn to you from the beginning because of your drive and sass, but now? Now I find myself drawn to your kind heart and ability to take care of people with food. I love how you're so focused but still take notice of others. I love how you push yourself past your fears and want to understand the things around you. I love how you take your work seriously and always want to suc-ceed. I love that you love your family and don't want to let them down."

He kissed the tip of her nose. "And I love how you have let me into your world, even if it was kicking and screaming."

She laughed, a tear slowly sliding down her cheek. "And I love how you wouldn't take no for an answer."

Antony's mouth shifted into that arrogant smirk she adored. "Those might be the sweetest words I've ever heard escape your lips." He brought his own lips, so close she could feel him when he spoke. "But sometimes actions are even more delicious."

Emory hummed in agreement as Antony took her mouth and her breath all in one fell swoop. The muttered grumblings of their surrounding audience seemed to fade away and Emory felt as if she could conquer the world, despite the exhaustion of her body and mind.

She'd been content without him in her life. She was pushing forward, if not at the pace she wanted, but still making progress. She had family, a career, and her cousins were wonderful friends to her. But somehow, this man who had started out as her competition, ended up making her stronger. *And without his help, I never would have been able to rebuild the gingerbread house or the display room. Who knew a little friendly competition could make life so much better?*

"Ummm...Emory?"

Emory ignored her cousin's question. Right now she was exactly where she wanted to be...and with whom.

"Em!"

Gasping, Emory finally separated from Antony. Her breathing was much too fast and her skin too warm, but she couldn't help but smile at him when he allowed her to pull back. "Sorry..." she breathed. "I got a little carried away."

Antony chuckled and kissed her forehead. "And yet I don't regret it a bit," he muttered under his breath.

"Sorry to interrupt such an..." Bella cleared her throat, "interesting moment, but you're going to have people showing up with their displays within a couple of hours." She looked Emory up and down. "I think we need to get ready."

Emory groaned and immediately rubbed her temples. "Yep. You're right. I'm on it."

Antony's hand went to her neck. "We're on it," he corrected.

Emory looked up at him. "Right. We're on it." She reached up and brushed his hair out of his eyes. "You better run home and get your bakery going or your customers will be wondering what happened."

His face fell slightly. "Hopefully I have customers."

A sharp pain hit her heart. "I forgot about that. What are you going to do?"

He shrugged and gave her his signature smirk. "First thing I'm going to do is take a shower. Then after work, I'm going to bring my own display over and see if you need help."

Emory opened her mouth to argue, but he gave her a quick kiss to keep her quiet.

"I'll worry about the bakery after Christmas. Maybe by then, whatever's happened will have cleared itself up."

Emory wasn't so sure, but she nodded anyway and made a mental note to herself. As soon as the hubbub at the inn calmed down, she would personally go figure out why his customers had deserted him. She knew most of the residents of the town and it shouldn't be too hard to figure out what was going on.

In a place as small as Seagull Cove, gossip spread faster than hot ganache on a cake.

"See you soon, beautiful," he said softly, leaving one last lingering kiss on her lips.

"Love you," Emory managed to whisper back as he turned to walk away.

Antony stopped and glanced back at her. "*I* love *you*," he echoed. With a wink, he disappeared and Emory found herself feeling cold.

She wasn't quite sure where exactly she and Antony were headed, but now that she'd experienced life with color and passion, she found what she'd had before lacking somehow, and she hoped she didn't have to go back to it anytime soon.

Except you have a job waiting for you in Seattle. What happens after New Year's? Chef Tyrell won't be understanding if you want more time off.

She sighed and rubbed her temples yet again. Lack of sleep and the still heavy weight of responsibility on her shoulders was causing her usual headaches to step up a notch.

"Come on, cuz," Bella said lightly. "You can kiss hot Italian guy in a little while. Right now...we've got a competition to win."

Emory laughed tiredly as Bella put her arm around her shoulders. "Oh? And will you be kissing hot Detective man as well?"

"Of course," Bella responded with a grin. "What good is a hunky guy if you can't cuddle up to him once in a while?"

Emory shrugged as they entered the kitchen. "I don't know. Opening pickle jars?"

Bella laughed. "I hate pickles."

"Then I suppose kissing is all that's left," Emory teased with a dramatic sigh.

"Darn right," Bella said proudly. "And don't you forget it."

After what I just went through? I don't think I will.

ANTONY COULDN'T CONCENTRATE on his work that morning. He snorted. "That's nothing new," he grumbled as he put an egg wash on the challah bread. "At least not since I met Emory."

A goofy smile broke out on his face as he thought of their confessions this morning. He hadn't meant to fall in love with her. It had just naturally happened. She'd caught his eye with her beauty, but now she held his heart with the rest of her. Her wit, her spark, her kindness, her courage, and even her work ethic.

There was nothing more attractive than a woman who wasn't afraid to get down and dirty. And the way she forgave Jim? Even to the point of offering him food and shelter? Antony shook his head. "Could a guy get any more lucky?"

"Hey, boss?"

Antony straightened and looked at Jennifer. "Yeah?"

"It's still slow out here. Did you need to run your entry over to the inn?"

Antony nodded, frustrated that business was still down. "Yeah." He looked down at his bread. "Can you pull this out when the timer goes off?"

Jennifer tapped her lips. "Geez. I don't know. Manual labor might be above my pay grade."

Laughing, Antony shook his head and stripped off his apron. "Thanks, Jen. I owe you one."

She grinned. "I take payments in cookies anytime."

"Done." He grabbed his jacket, then headed for the walk-in cooler. "Just don't eat any in front of the customer, 'kay?"

"As if I would," she scoffed. "What kind of Neanderthal do you take me for?"

"A hungry teenager?"

She scrunched up her nose. "Point taken."

Antony grinned again. He had a lot of siblings, but they were all older. Having Jen as the little sister type was more fun than he'd imagined. Taking a deep breath, he faced his creation for the competition. He'd slaved over this thing and lost many hours of sleep trying to finish it. He should have been working on it during the evenings, but since they were becoming his time with Emory, he'd started staying up into the wee hours of the morning in order to get it done.

The grand tree in front of him, however, was absolutely done. And he was particularly proud of his work. The modeling chocolate, edible glitter, and sugar work were some of his best. The tree was built from gingerbread, but the decorations were not. Snow dripped from every branch, while sugar and glitter gave the whole piece an ethereal glow, as if the moon was shining down on it. The ornaments were made out of blown sugar and they had become fragile works of art unto themselves.

"Now I just have to get it to Gingerbread Inn in one piece," he muttered to himself.

"Want me to back the van up to the door?" Jen called from the cooler entrance.

"Yeah..." Antony scratched his chin. "I should have thought of that."

"Toss 'em here." Jennifer held out her hand and easily caught the keys. "I'll come back in and help with the cart. Hang tight."

While she was gone, Antony pulled a pastry cart over and very carefully lifted his beautiful creation onto it. Then, with Jen's help he got it loaded and strapped down.

"Good luck!" she called out as he got inside the vehicle. "It's amazing!"

Antony grinned. "Thanks! Here's hoping the judges think the same thing." Putting the van into drive, he slowly started out. "And I wouldn't be upset if Emory did too."

It only took ten minutes to get to the inn, but it might as well have been a marathon. Antony could feel sweat trickling down his back as he worried over every bump in the road and prayed that his structure had held tight the whole time. He still felt that winning the Gingerbread Inn contest would do good things for his business, but his motivations had completely shifted. He had almost pulled out of the festival when he and Emory had been dating for a while and he knew his feelings were more serious than they had been with every other woman.

He didn't want to compete against her. However, Emory was so strong and he *knew* that if he backed out, she would take it as a personal insult. After hearing her say she loved him this morning, he knew that it didn't matter who won, they would still be okay.

He carefully unloaded and then drug his cart around back so they could take the easier route to the display room. Hopping up the back steps to his private entrance, Antony knocked on the kitchen door. When Emory answered with a wide smile, he immediately grabbed her and pulled her in for a searing kiss.

When she pulled back, they were both breathing heavily. "Did you run out of sugar again?" she teased breathlessly.

Antony chuckled and kissed her forehead. "My supply has a nasty habit of disappearing as soon as you're out of sight."

Emory sighed and settled her head on his chest. "Remind me to give you something to remember me by when you have to leave."

"Done." He kissed her forehead again. "I brought my display. Can we take it through here so it's easier to get to the display room?"

"Oh! Of course." Emory stepped away from him and her eyes went to his cart. "Antony..." she breathed. Stumbling down the steps, she went to his gingerbread tree. Her hands covered her mouth and were trembling.

Antony watched her warily, hoping she wasn't upset. He didn't quite understand her reaction but hoped it was a good one.

She shook her head. "It's amazing," she said in a barely audible voice. Her misty eyes went to him, shining with love and pride, and Antony relaxed. "You are so insanely talented!"

His lips quirked up on one side of his mouth. "No more than you."

She shook her head. "I can't do anything like this." Her eyes went back to the tree. "It's no wonder you went to school for art. There's a life to your work that I haven't mastered yet."

Antony came up behind her and wrapped his arms around her waist, resting his chin against her head. "Maybe so, but the most beautiful piece of art in my life is one I had no hand in making. I can't take credit for God's work." He kissed her hair.

"Cheesy, cheesy, cheesy," Emory said, though Antony could hear the thickness in her voice.

"Just like before, you left it hanging. Someone had to utilize it," he quipped, referring to the pun he'd pulled on their first date.

She spun in his arms. "Well, thank you for such a wonderful compliment. But we need to get your stunning creation inside before it rains and is ruined."

Antony glanced up at the dark clouds. "Sounds like a plan. Can you hold the door?'

"Yeah, hang on." She dashed inside and returned a few minutes later with Enoch at her side.

"Need some help?" Enoch asked with a grin.

"Another set of hands would be great, thanks," Antony said.

Enoch whistled low under his breath. "Mrs. Pearson isn't going to like this at all." He smiled widely. "Which is awesome."

Antony chuckled. "Well, if we don't get it inside, nobody is going to like it."

"Right. On it."

Together the two men carried the large display inside and got it settled into the correct spot in the village.

"Whew." Antony wiped at his brow. "I'm so glad to have that done."

Emory wrapped her arms around his waist. "I can't imagine how much time that took you." She shook her head again. "Seriously. I've never seen anything like it."

Antony's left arm went around her. "You're going to inflate my already big ego."

She laughed. "In this case, I have to say, I think it's deserved."

"I'll remember that," he quipped.

"I didn't doubt it for a moment."

CHAPTER 16

E mory held her breath.

"We'd like to thank everyone for coming to the annual Gingerbread Festival!" Bella called from her spot in the center of the room. She nodded and smiled as everyone clapped. "With Grandma Claire passing the baton to us three women, there were, as you can imagine, several ups and down along the way to get here tonight."

Emory's breath whooshed out when Antony's arms went around her waist.

"Nervous?" he whispered in her ear, taking a second to nip the lobe.

She gasped. "Antony!" she scolded, looking around to see if anyone was paying attention. "The only thing I'm nervous about is people seeing you do that in public."

He chuckled and she savored the sound as it resonated through his chest into her back. "Would you rather I did it in private?"

"You are so naughty!" Emory scolded, shaking her head.

"Someone has to be in this relationship," he answered. "Otherwise we would never have any fun."

Emory finally laughed. "You're too much. I don't know what to do with you."

"Just keep loving me," he whispered, his voice low and serious. "And say you'll stay in Seagull Cove, rather than head back to Seattle."

Emory felt her eyes grow wide and she froze at his suggestion.

"Are you ready to hear the winners?" Bella called out.

The crowd roared their approval.

"Breathe, sweetheart," Antony said. "And get ready to smile."

Emory forced her lungs into motion. She wasn't sure what she was more nervous about. The winners of the competition or answering

Antony's suggestion. She hadn't been able to think much past this moment in time, though she knew the future would have to be addressed.

But was she ready to give up her job for this man? What if things didn't work out between them? Seagull Cove wasn't very large and she wasn't sure if they could live together if they broke up.

"Let's start with third place," Bella continued. She pulled out an envelope. "Drum roll, please!"

A chunk of the audience began to hit their thighs, creating a thumping undertone.

Bella preened under the attention and Emory couldn't help but grin, her tension easing slightly.

"Third place goes to...Mrs. Pearson!" Bella called out. She held up a large ribbon.

The disgruntled old woman stormed her way to the front and grabbed the ribbon, glaring at the crowd.

"Congratulations!" Bella called out, grinning widely as Mrs. Pearson stalked away. Bella met Emory's gaze and winked.

Emory tsked her tongue and shook her head. "Never poke the bear," she muttered.

Antony gave her a squeeze. "I don't think poking the bear makes much of a difference. She's grumpy either way. And besides, she got what she wanted, right? She said she refused to take home second place this year."

Emory had to give him that. Nothing seemed to make Mrs. Pearson happy. In fact, she seemed to delight in the bringing down of others. *What a sad, lonely existence that must be.*

"Second place goes to..." Bella's face lit up. "EMORY MASON!" She squealed and bounced on her toes. "Emory! Come here!"

Emory smiled as the crowd roared and Antony turned and gave her a short, fierce kiss before pushing her toward Bella. Despite the happy look she was trying to sport, Emory was breaking inside. Her grandmother's streak was broken. And it was her fault.

"Congrats!" Bella shouted, grabbing Emory in a tight hug. "You are so amazing!" she whispered in Emory's ear.

Emory backed up and nodded. "Thank you," she responded, taking the offered ribbon.

Bella held tightly to her arm. "Your competition this year was far different than anything Grandma ever went up against," Bella said with a serious expression. "Be proud of yourself, Emory. You overcame a lot to get here and still won."

Emory nodded, but didn't say anything else. She turned to walk back to Antony and suddenly stopped. Without waiting to hear Bella announce it, Emory knew exactly who had won, and she knew it was well deserved.

Antony, with his messy hair and intense gray eyes. Antony, with his heart of gold and his arrogant smirk. Antony, with his amazing artistic skill and delicious baking abilities. Emory had never stood a chance. No amount of tiny lattice work or dripping icicles could make up for the passion and life in his work.

Rather than feeling worse about the revelation, Emory felt a surge of pride and gratitude. This amazing man was hers. He was choosing to share his time, energy, and even his kitchen with her. She knew all she would have to do was ask and Antony would be more than happy to share his art with her as well. And she suddenly felt ravenously hungry for it. For him.

"ANTONY HARRISON!" Bella screamed. "Your amazing Gingerbread Christmas Tree has taken the prize!"

Antony began to walk toward Bella, passing Emory along the way. He paused, his eyes concerned. "Are you all right?" he asked quietly, glancing around at the crowd and nodding at their cheers.

"Never better," Emory said, smiling back. She stood on tiptoe and kissed his jawline. "Hurry back to me so we can talk about your comment earlier."

His eyes widened and began to flash with his usual mischief. "Stay put, Em, baby. I'm coming."

Emory laughed lightly and walked back to the outside of the crowd as Antony received his prize and congratulations. It was several minutes before he made his way back to her side, and several more before they could actually speak to each other.

It seemed that everyone in the room wanted to congratulate the two on their prizes and talk about the wonderful creations.

Antony must have decided he had had enough, because he eventually took Emory's hand, excused them from the group, and marched her out into the hallway. He tugged on her hard and swung Emory around until her back was against the wall behind the door. Putting his hands on either side of her head, he caged her in and brought his face down to hers. "Now...you hinted at something earlier that I'm very interested in hearing."

Emory grinned and slowly slid her hands up his chest, enjoying the shiver that went through him, then wrapped her arms around his neck. "I was thinking a couple of things," she said, kissing his chin.

"Care to share?" he asked, his voice low and husky.

"One...we need to celebrate your win."

"*Our* wins," he responded.

"Our wins," Emory corrected, kissing just beside his lips.

"And the other?"

"Second...I was thinking I could ask Grandma if I could stay on as her permanent kitchen manager."

Antony's breathing grew slightly ragged. "Do you mean it?"

She leaned back just enough to see his face. "If you want me to."

"And what do you want?"

She grinned, finally knowing exactly how to answer this question. "I want freedom to bake...and you."

"Then this plan sounds perfect," he managed to get out before taking her mouth in their usual dance.

Yes, it does...

ANTONY HAD TASTED FOOD from Italy and all over America, but he had yet to find anything that satisfied him the way Emory did. He kept his hands on the wall, fighting the urge to pull her into his body and devour her. She was under his skin in a way he hoped never changed.

A throat cleared at his side and Antony cursed inside his head. He was far from ready to be done with his little minx, but they were at a very public party and it was going to be impossible to have her to himself for very long.

Reluctantly, Antony pulled back and looked at the intruder. "Hello, Sheriff Davidson."

Emory gasped and buried her face in his chest. "Oh my gosh. Could this get any more embarrassing?"

"It could have been your grandmother," Antony quipped. "Or my mother."

"We're here," Claire piped up, pushing the sheriff out of the way.

Antony grinned unrepentantly when his mother stood behind Claire with her arms folded over her chest. "Hello, Mom."

She tsked her tongue. "I taught you better manners."

He shrugged and wrapped Emory in his arms. "The future Mrs. Harrison seems to wipe my mind of any rational thought," he retorted.

Emory gasped even more loudly. "What?" she screeched.

He looked down and kissed her nose. "Don't deny that we both know it's coming."

She raised a sassy eyebrow at him. "Until I actually hear a proposal, I will categorically deny that."

"Guess I'll have to make it good," he responded.

"Of course you should," his mother interrupted. "She deserves to be romanced, not eaten."

Antony made a face. "The other is more fun," he said in an aside, then winced and laughed when Emory elbowed him.

Sheriff Davidson cleared his throat again, but there was definite laughter in the sound as he drew the group's attention. "I just thought I'd let you know that we've finished a bit of our detective work."

Emory straightened, growing serious. "What can you tell us, Sheriff?"

Sheriff Davidson sighed. "We found the social worker and she's actually on her way here right now." He looked at his watch. "Should be here soon, by my estimation."

Emory nodded, then leaned into Antony's chest and he wrapped his arms around her. "I'm sure that's the right thing, but I still hate to send him back."

Antony kissed the top of her head, understanding her feelings. "He needs to go to school and be with friends," he reassured her. "I'm sure they'll take better care of him this time around."

"Let's hope so."

"On the other hand, little Jim says he didn't have anything to do with open doors or leaving garden tools in the grass."

Emory groaned. "Do you think it's the same person who destroyed the display room?"

Sheriff Davidson shrugged. "Could be. But it could also be a neglectful guest or worker. The two problems don't necessarily have to do with each other."

"I suppose so," Emory muttered. "But I still don't like it."

The sheriff nodded. "Me either."

Antony had to agree. He would be glad when everything was solved once and for all.

The ringing of the doorbell surprised the whole party and they turned toward the sound.

"I'll get it," Emory said when no one else moved. The group followed her as she headed to the foyer and opened the door. "Hello, welcome to the Cliffside Bed and Breakfast, also known as Gingerbread Inn. Can I help you?"

"Yes...I'm Susan Nettles. I'm a social worker. I've come for Jimmy Harmon."

Emory looked over her shoulder to the group and Antony could see the sadness in her eyes. She turned back to the door. "Come on in," she urged. "Jim is at a party at the moment, but we can go get him."

Two women came inside as Emory closed the door.

Emory turned to the second woman. "I'm sorry. I should have introduced myself. I'm Emory Mason, the baker here at the inn. And you are?" She held out her hand.

"MISS EUGENE!" Jim's voice echoed through the large space and he practically slid across the floor in his sprint to reach the elderly woman.

"Jimmy!" The woman opened her arms and Mrs. Nettles had to help hold her up as the boy slammed into his caretaker.

"I missed you," he sobbed into her shoulder.

"I missed you too," Miss Eugene whispered back. "You don't know how much." She pulled back and cupped his face. "What were you thinking, running away? Didn't we have a good life?"

He nodded and wiped at his running nose. "Yeah, but they took me away. She said you were sick." He pointed to Mrs. Nettles.

Miss Eugene clucked her tongue. "It wasn't going to last very long. As you can see, I'm all better." She gave him a stern look. "If you had waited around, you would have seen that."

"I'm sorry," he said, hanging his head. "I was just so tired of being with people who don't care."

"Never mind that," Miss Eugene hurried to say. "We're back together and tomorrow is Christmas. We need to get going so we can celebrate properly."

Emory's misty eyes met Antony's and he smiled at her. It was hard not to be emotional at the sweet reunion and the Christmas miracle that was happening before their eyes.

"Actually," Emory said, stepping forward, "if you're up for it, we have a gingerbread festival going on right down the hall. Everyone is welcome and I can guarantee that the sweets and hot chocolate are some of the best you'll ever try."

"Is that so?" Miss Eugene asked playfully. She looked down at Jim. "Can you vouch for her claim?"

He grinned. "Yeah. I already tried almost everything."

She sighed. "Of course you did." Straightening, she turned back to the group. "First of all, thank you for taking care of my Jimmy boy. I understand he gave you a bit of a fright, but I'm grateful you saw fit to help him out instead of turning him in." She cleared her throat. "And I suppose if Mrs. Nettles is willing, staying for a party might be a wonderful way to spend our Christmas Eve."

Mrs. Nettles shrugged. "I could use a good cookie or two."

Claire stepped forward with Antony's mother right behind her. Antony grinned as he realized those two were becoming thick as thieves. "Then you just come with us," Claire said soothingly. "We'll make sure you're taken care of. Between what my granddaughter bakes and her boyfriend, we'll put a few pounds on you before you leave tonight."

The group chuckled and slowly worked their way down the hall.

Antony walked over to Emory and wrapped an arm around her shoulders. "You're amazing," he said.

"I'm gonna miss the squirt," she said sadly, watching the group go. "Now who will steal my treats?"

"Oh, you just wait, sweetheart," Antony said, purposefully dropping his voice. He turned her around to face him. "I'm planning to steal sugar from you for years to come."

"Promises, promises," she teased right before he kept her mouth busy with much more enjoyable activities.

EPILOGUE

"I've got a surprise for you," Antony said in a low voice.

Emory looked over her shoulder at him and grinned. "You do, huh? Should I be concerned?"

He rested the box he was holding on his hip and put his other hand on his chest. "What kind of a question is that? Have I ever given you a bad surprise?"

Emory turned fully around and rested her hands on her hips. "Come to think of it, I'm not sure you've ever given me a surprise." She raised her eyebrows. "So now I'm really worried."

Antony chuckled, a sound that Emory absolutely adored, and stepped forward to kiss the end of her nose. "Then maybe it's time I start." He stepped past her to the counter she was working at and dropped his box on it. A rattling sound came from inside, piquing Emory's interest.

She leaned around his shoulder. "What's in there?"

"Oh...so now you're interested?" he teased.

Emory rolled her eyes. "Fine...I won't ask."

Antony reached out and pulled her in-between him and the counter. It was one of Emory's favorite places. They did a lot of baking that way...baking that inevitably led to kissing, which was Emory's favorite dessert.

He made her face forward and brought his mouth down to her ear. "Open the box."

Emory shook her head with a smile and followed his orders. Inside was a tangled mass of silver and she laughed. "Oh my goodness! What did you find?" She dug around. "How many cookie cutters are in here?"

Antony shrugged. "I didn't count. But I couldn't pass them up."

She spun around and wrapped her arms around his neck. These last few months with him had been amazing. With the stress of the gingerbread festival over and the tourism trade picking up, Emory had never been happier. She was free to bake, experiment, and create to her heart's desire. And her time with Antony had become the most precious part of her day. They often worked in each other's kitchens, and had created several new recipes together, which were quickly becoming town favorites.

After the festival, his business had been bursting at the seams and the information had quickly been revealed that Mrs. Pearson had been behind his slowdown. After a visit from Sheriff Davidson, the elderly woman had suddenly disappeared. It was rumored she went to live with a daughter further down the coast.

"Thank you," she said before quickly kissing him. "You know I love cookie cutters."

"I know," he boasted. Then he turned her around again. "But you haven't looked to see what they are."

"Who cares what they are?" she asked. "They're from you and that makes them all the more wonderful."

"Em," he said in exasperation. "Look at them."

"Fine, fine." She began to pull them out. "Oooh! Letters! How fun. Is the whole alphabet in here?"

"Nope."

She frowned as she began to pull out multiples of the same letter. "Uh..."

Antony put his hands over hers and helped finish unpacking the box. Then he tossed it aside and guided her in combining the letters into a sentence...or rather a question.

Emory's breath began to grow shallow and her eyes filled with tears. "Antony..." When he stepped away from her back, she turned to find him down on his knee with a velvet box in his palm.

"Emory Claire Mason," he began. "I knew I had to get to know you from the moment you walked into my bakery. Your spunk and beauty were the first things that drew me to your side, but it was your goodness and tenacity that kept me there. You are amazing. An amazing artist, baker, friend, granddaughter, girlfriend...and kisser." He winked and she snorted laughter through her tears.

"I know that myself and my kitchen will never be the same unless I have you permanently in my life. Will you make me the most blessed man alive and agree to be my baking partner and wife?"

Emory nodded her head immediately. "Yes," she whispered. "YES!" She tugged on his hand. "Stand up so I can hug you!"

He laughed and stood on his feet, but held her off just long enough to put the ring on her finger before she leapt onto him.

Emory let her tears flow as she clung to his neck. "And just for the record, I find you amazing as well. Stubborn, arrogant, cocky, and absolutely, completely...amazing."

Antony squeezed her tighter. "Do you like the ring?" he whispered in her ear.

"I love it."

He laughed. "Have you even looked at it?"

Emory shook her head. "No."

"Em!" He pushed her back with a playful glare. "I spent a lot of time working on that ring."

She smiled and finally looked down at her hand, only to gasp. "Oh, Antony!" The large diamond solitaire in the middle had a long line of smaller diamonds swirling around it and running down her finger. It was bold and stunning and everything she could have ever dreamed of. "It's perfect."

He pulled her back into his chest, kissing her forehead. "It had to be. It was for the perfect woman."

She laughed at his quip and settled her head against his chest. "I never would have imagined that one Christmas at Gingerbread Inn would have led me to this," she murmured.

"Hey, that wasn't just any Christmas! How many people do you know who get their very own baker under the tree?" He laughed and buried his face in her hair. "And you didn't just get a baker for Christmas, you got one for life." She could feel him grin. "And guess what that means?"

"What?"

"It now means you'll never have a headache again."

"Oh, really?" She leaned back to look him in the eye. "Why's that?"

"Because now I can do this whenever I want." When his lips met hers, Emory knew he was right. There was absolutely nothing his delicious kisses couldn't fix, and that included her worries and stress.

She clung to him, eager for the future that they would conquer together and grateful that a Christmas season she had been dreading had turned out to be the most amazing of them all.

THE END
(Check out "Her Christmas Detective" to read Bella and Hank's story!)

Other Books by Laura Ann

THE GINGERBREAD INN [1]
"Her Christmas Handyman"[2]
"Her Christmas Baker"[3]
"Her Christmas Detective"[4]
SAGEBRUSH RANCH
When city girls meet cowboys,
the shenanigans are epic.
Books 1-6[5]
LOCKWOOD INDUSTRIES
The Lockwood triplets started a personal security business.
Little did they know it would double as a matchmaking business!
Books 1-6[6]
OVERNIGHT BILLIONAIRE BACHELORS
Three brothers become overnight billionaires.
Will they discover that love is the real treasure?
Books 1-5[7]
IT'S ALL ABOUT THE MISTLETOE
When 6 friends brings fake dates to the Holiday Ball,
mayhem, mistletoe and love win the day!

---

1. https://www.amazon.com/gp/product/B08N4JD51P?ref_=dbs_p_mng_rwt_ser_shvlr&store-Type=ebooks

2. https://www.amazon.com/dp/B08MZ3NKRM

3. https://www.amazon.com/dp/B08N4Q5KH2

4. https://www.amazon.com/dp/B08N3NKDHK

5. https://www.amazon.com/gp/product/B089YPCF6X?ref_=dbs_r_series&storeType=ebooks

6. https://www.amazon.com/gp/product/B083Z49VL3?ref_=dbs_r_series&storeType=ebooks

7. https://www.amazon.com/gp/product/B07RJZL29J?ref_=dbs_r_series&storeType=ebooks

Books 1-6[8]
MIDDLETON PREP
If you enjoy fairy tale romance,
these sweet, contemporary retellings are for you!
Books 1-9[9]

---

8. https://www.amazon.com/gp/product/B082F8FTHY?ref_=dbs_r_series&storeType=ebooks

9. https://www.amazon.com/gp/product/B07DYCWRQL?ref_=dbs_r_series&store-
    Type=ebooks